A TEAR in the OCEAN

A Tear in the OCEAN

COMPANION TO *A CRACK IN THE SEA*

H. M. BOUWMAN

ILLUSTRATIONS BY *YUKO SHIMIZU*

putnam

G. P. Putnam's Sons

G. P. Putnam's Sons
an imprint of Penguin Random House LLC
375 Hudson Street
New York, NY 10014

Copyright © 2019 by H. M. Bouwman.
Illustrations copyright © 2019 by Yuko Shimizu.

G. P. Putnam's Sons is a registered trademark of Penguin Random House LLC.
Library of Congress Cataloging-in-Publication Data
Names: Bouwman, H. M., author. | Shimizu, Yuko, 1965– illustrator.
Title: A tear in the ocean / H. M. Bouwman; illustrations, Yuko Shimizu.
Description: New York, NY: G. P. Putnam's Sons, [2019]
Summary: Told in two voices and times, Artie runs away from her abusive stepfather and Rayel from an arranged marriage, and both find adventure on the high seas beyond Raftworld.
Identifiers: LCCN 2018025578 | ISBN 9780399545221 (hardback) |
ISBN 9780399545238 (ebook)
Subjects: | CYAC: Fantasy. | BISAC: JUVENILE FICTION / Fantasy & Magic. | JUVENILE FICTION / Action & Adventure / General. | JUVENILE FICTION / Historical / General.
Classification: LCC PZ7.B6713 Te 2019 | DDC [Fic]—dc23
LC record available at https://lccn.loc.gov/2018025578

Printed in the United States of America.
ISBN 9780399545221
10 9 8 7 6 5 4 3 2 1

Text set in Maxime Std.

This is a work of fiction. Names, characters, places, and incidents either are the product of the author's imagination or are used fictitiously, and any resemblance to actual persons, living or dead, businesses, companies, events, or locales is entirely coincidental.

For my dad, stained glass through which the light shines.

PART ONE

Explorer, Hero, Runaway

PUTNAM. THE PRESENT: 1949.

1

*P*UTNAM WATCHED a tattered girl about his own age at the edge of the bonfire. For the past hour, she'd hovered in the shadows just outside the glow of the flames. Her face would pop into the light briefly, then snuff itself out again, only to reappear several moments later, then disappear, like a candle being lit and immediately blown out.

She'd been circling the fire, when Putnam, looking for the best spot to listen and watch, noticed her. But she stopped moving about the same time he did, not quite across the fire from him. As he listened to Jupiter, the storyteller, entertain the people with a funny tale about the time long ago when they tried to grow mangoes on Raftworld (sadly, there was not enough dirt for the trees to root in), Putnam's eyes flicked again and again to the spot where the girl's face would suddenly jut out of the darkness and then fall back into it. She didn't seem to realize she could be seen, and no one but Putnam noticed her.

Part of the reason she stood out to Putnam so much was her obvious wish not to be seen. Putnam understood that desire; he was trying to stay out of the light, too. Everyone expected so much of him—the Raft King's son! the next king of Raftworld!—and sometimes he just needed to get away. Maybe this girl had some of the same feelings. Maybe *her* so-called friends were always following her around, too, hoping for favors and being nice to her because of who her dad was.

Or maybe not. Putnam squinted at the girl through the smoke. An Islander, she had the lighter brown skin and straight hair and stocky body that was the classic Tathenlander look. But unlike the other Islanders, she wasn't spiffed up, wearing her best clothes for the party; she acted as if she wasn't even supposed to be at the party.

She made Putnam think of the story the Island's former storyteller (now dead) had told the last time Raftworld had visited the Islands, when he'd been only two—ten years ago. He didn't remember the actual words the Island storyteller had used, of course, but Jupiter had retold the tale since then: a poor orphan girl who'd been forced to work for her rich, hateful stepmother and who, when the prince threw a party, snuck in and eventually captured the prince's heart. Except—Putnam reminded himself—that girl had been given a ball gown and fragile gypsum slippers when she snuck into the ball, and this girl was here simply as herself. She wasn't likely to win a prince's heart the way she looked and acted.

He smiled at the next thought: technically, he supposed, he was the prince in the story. Though no one called him by that title, he was in fact the Raft King's only child. So if he were to follow the story's plot, he should chase this girl down and grab one of her shoes . . . if she *had* shoes . . .

The girl materialized one more time, the firelight playing on a set of bruises on one side of her face. Jupiter had moved on to a more serious story: how the Raftworlders' ancestor Venus escaped from being enslaved. And this time, as Jupiter the storyteller explained the moment of decision, the choice Venus made, the tattered girl emerged and didn't snuff right back into darkness. This time her face stayed in the light, entranced as she was by the story. And there was something in the fire's glow that made her look—not pretty, no, nor healthy nor well cared for—but full of determination and spirit and energy. Just for that moment.

Jupiter's story ended, and she vanished. Vivid in the fire's flickering light one moment, gone the next.

A big hand descended on Putnam's shoulder, and for one brief second he thought it was the girl, coming after him instead of waiting for him to chase her down and steal her shoe. But as soon as that thought flitted into his head, he knew it was wrong. First of all, the hand was too large and heavy.

"It's time." His father, of course—tall, thin, and a little stooped, in the dark red cloak he wore for official events, his graying beard closely trimmed.

Putnam nodded. He already stood in the back of the crowd; he didn't even have to jostle anyone to leave. For a moment he wondered what it would be like to just vanish, like that girl.

"Are you coming?" asked his father. "Your first Session. Let's not be late."

Putnam nodded again and hurried after the old man.

THE TRADING SESSION—usually just called "the Session"—was the biggest meeting in the entire world, which wasn't saying much, as the world was small, at least where people were concerned. The Session, which lasted for several days with long breaks for the delegates to attend parties and socialize, happened every decade or so, whenever the floating nation of Raftworld arrived in the course of its usual travels to the islands of Tathenland and the big island of Tathenn and its capital city of Baytown. Then the Raftworlders and Islanders got together for a week or more of parties and storytelling and singing . . . and trading. The Raft King and the Island's governor—and other important people—attended meetings, exchanged important information, made deals. This year, the Raft King had said that now that he was twelve, Putnam was old enough to go to the meetings. As if that was a privilege. It *was*, but the other delegates were grown-ups. And the meeting was all *talking*.

Putnam sat in the back corner of the room next to a convenient tray of cookies, rather than at the delegates' table, which was only big enough for the eight women and men—four from each country—who ran the Session. He was supposed to be listening and learning. He nibbled and made crumbs and tried—he really did—to pay attention.

But the day had been long, and his mind wandered, and after an hour or more of discussions of flour and wool and embroidered cloth and hydraulic engines and so many other things, his eyes drooped. Just before he slid into deep sleep, he remembered himself and snapped back, shifting suddenly in his chair and crumbling the cookie still clutched in his hand.

Eight heads rotated toward him, conversation stalling for a moment. "Sorry," he muttered, feeling foolish, as they turned back to discussion. He knew he should be listening deeply at his first Session, maybe even saying something important—but barring that, at least he should *look* like he was listening. He pinched his leg, hard, and sat up straighter, shoving the broken cookie into his mouth and chewing vigorously.

And the pinching and chewing helped. He felt less tired, at least for the moment.

Until he realized what the Session leaders were talking about now: the ocean. A cloud of gloom settled over the room, and Putnam could tell that, long before the topic was introduced, everyone had been thinking about the water. It had been turning salty—slowly, steadily—for some time. But no matter how often Raftworld advisors told the king, he brushed off the problem. Even when his own son brought it up, the king refused to discuss it. It was in their imaginations, he said. It would get better on its own, he said. It was a normal fluctuation, he said.

In his corner, Putnam sat up straighter. Maybe now his father would be forced to listen.

"There's no doubt at all in our minds," one of the Islanders said stubbornly to Putnam's father. "You don't see it as much because you're always moving around."

"You make it sound like *moving around* is a bad thing. What are you trying to say about us?" asked a Raftworlder, one of his father's advisors.

"Now, that isn't what's meant at all," said the governor in a soothing voice. She was much younger than Putnam's father, who'd been old already when Putnam was born. Tiny compared to Putnam's father, she sat straight in her seat, as if trying to look taller. Her dark braids wrapped around her head like a crown and shone in the light.

She continued. "We're only saying that we *see* the changes more, situated as we are in one location. In the past few years, the fish have been leaving us, heading north. The algae is dying. We know that our capital is better off than other places on Tathenn—it's much worse on the southern shores. We can't ask the fish like you can"—she paused as if waiting for the king to say something, but he didn't speak—"but even so, we can read the water pretty well. The changes aren't good."

She waited again, then said, "What *did* the fish say?"

"They didn't answer any questions."

The young governor's face fell.

"The water's going bad. You can taste that yourself," added one of the governor's advisors, folding his arms over his chest and nodding at the pitcher on the table.

Several Raftworlders leaned forward to add their thoughts. One said, "It does seem worse the farther south we get. When we were north earlier this year, remember how fresh—"

Putnam's father held up his long, thin hand, and everyone stopped for the Raft King to speak. "The water here has changed, it's true. I can tell from our last visit that it's different. Kind of salty, yes?" The governor's advisor nodded, as did the other Islanders in the room. "But what you have to ask yourself is this: is it maybe just a natural swing in the order of things? Or maybe because of something you've done here on the Islands?"

"And it's affected the entire ocean?" asked the governor. "Your advisor just said the water is different the world over."

The king shrugged, his face blank of expression. "He said it *seemed* that way. And other times it seems fine. We need to study it more to be sure. That's my suggestion: that we form committees. Maybe you Islanders can take samples and track any changes over time—compare data for a few years and see if it's really getting salty and, if so, how bad it is. And when Raftworld travels, we'll take samples at key locations as well, so that the next time we stop at those places, we can also compare."

"The next time? You mean ten years from now, when you circle back?"

"It's not always ten years. There are some places we visit every five or six years. It really depends."

"But the water's gone from good to bad in just a few years. And you're arguing for a decade of testing," said one of the Islanders, a gray-haired woman who looked about as old as the king. "Before we even do anything."

The Raft King paused as if thinking about his answer, and then nodded. "Raftworld moves, but we move slowly. It's what has kept us safe all these years. We don't rush."

Putnam, sitting off to the side with the cookies, could see the looks on the Islanders' faces and in their stiff shoulders and bodies: frustration and worry. He could see, more faintly, similar looks in the Raftworlders' faces—everyone's but his father's. This idea of moving slowly was . . . too *slow*. Obviously something needed to be done, and everyone but the Raft King was ready to do it.

"If we don't take action . . . ," said the young governor of the Islands. She didn't finish the sentence. She didn't have to. They all depended on the ocean—Raftworld and Tathenland— for food, for water. For everything.

One of the Raft King's advisors broke the silence. "Well, this is a topic we should return to. Tomorrow morning?" She stood, stretching her lower back and smiling a little too big. "There is, after all, a party tonight to attend."

Others stood, too, but not the governor, who spread her hands on the table, palms down, almost as if the table were trying to fly off. She didn't smile, either. "We're not done here."

"We'll talk about it again." One of the governor's own advisors, an elderly man who wore the old-fashioned Island clothing even down to the luck pouch around his neck, patted her shoulder. "Tomorrow, when we're fresh."

Everyone filed out of the room except the governor and her elderly advisor, his hand still on her shoulder. Putnam, following the others out, turned in time to see the governor look up at the old man, her face strained.

"We'll *talk* tomorrow," she said.

"And then do something," her advisor said.

"Sure," she said, unconvinced. "If we stall long enough, pretending nothing is horribly wrong and forming *committees*"—she said the word as if it tasted bitter—"it will be just as bad as if we ignore it altogether. The sea is *dying*. And then we die, too."

The old Island man's hand flexed in a tight grip, then loosened. He smoothed her hair down, as if he were her father and she a young child. It occurred to Putnam that maybe he *was* her father. "I know," he said in a low voice. "If Raftworld ignores the problem, we'll have to figure it out on our own."

"The problem is coming from the south. We need explorers, scientists, *people*—to sail south, find out what's causing this. Fix it."

The old man nodded.

"But without ocean boats or seafaring folks—"

"I know."

"We needed Raftworld. They were our best hope, and they're saying no."

"It does sound that way. But maybe tomorrow..."

At the same moment they seemed to realize Putnam was still there, and as they turned to him, he muttered, "Excuse me," and stumbled out of the room.

Was this what a Session was? A place to avoid the real problems of the world? And was this who his father was? Someone too slow-moving or too scared to jump in and fix things?

PUTNAM CAUGHT up to his father as the older man neared the large tent that had been set aside for him. When Raftworld visited, the people of the Islands built tents for them

to stay in, dotted all along the beach, large and elaborate and brightly colored inside and out.

The Raft King's tent, once you were through the door flap, was lofty enough for a tall man to stand and reach for the ceiling without touching it, and it was hung with tapestries depicting many scenes from Island history: the original Islanders and their close-knit fishing villages; the three ships that capsized there hundreds of years ago, bringing so many immigrants from the other world; the fever, a few decades later, that killed off so many of these immigrants and their descendants; the nation that emerged from this and other disasters to become the Tathenland they all knew today. There was even a panel of cloth that showed Raftworld visiting, bringing goods to trade and occasional volunteers to move to the Islands.

Placed around the interior of the tent were a portable stove for heat, benches and pillows to sit and sleep on, and blankets to fight off any chill. Draperies could be closed for privacy—Putnam's own room was a curtained nook toward the back of the tent, also filled with pillows and cushions. Once he'd gotten used to the earth not moving beneath him, he liked it. A lot.

The Raft King turned to Putnam, and Putnam felt a surge of anger: how ancient his father was! And how set in his ways! He'd always been so large and impressive—but now, suddenly, he seemed shrunken. There were wrinkles around his eyes, and the gray was migrating up from his beard and invading his temples.

"What is it?" the old man asked mildly. He held the flap open for Putnam to enter, gesturing for him to go first.

Except for them, the tent was empty. "What's wrong?" the king asked. "Something's bothering you."

"The meeting," said Putnam. "People are worried about the ocean. And you're not doing anything."

The king smiled. "At least I need never fear that my son will hold things inside and not tell me what's bothering him."

"I'm serious."

"So am I. But, you want to know what I'm going to do." He sat on a padded bench and tapped the seat next to him for Putnam to sit.

Putnam stayed standing. When was his dad going to admit he was wrong and offer to take action? Everyone always said how thoughtful the king was, how good he was at listening to everyone, and Putnam used to think these were compliments. But now he knew: his dad was stalling. It was humiliating to have people think that Raftworld was a nation that didn't *do* things, that ignored problems. A nation that just floated at sea.

His father shrugged. "We're going to move carefully and deliberately. As we always do."

"This is an emergency."

"It's not."

"The Islanders can't move north when the water gets bad in their country. And it'll become an emergency for us, too, eventually. Because eventually *all* the water could go bad. Don't we want to fix it before that happens?"

"We don't know how to fix it. Whatever you mean by *it*."

His father was so irritating! Putnam again felt the hot embarrassment of overhearing the governor's conversation with her elderly advisor, and the advisor's promise to do something even if Raftworld wouldn't help.

They probably thought he was just like his dad. Unwilling.

No, Putnam thought. *Raftworld* will *help. But—*

"You said the fish didn't answer."

The Raft King's face shifted, for a quick moment, into something that looked like stubbornness, and then it was gone. He looked at the floor, avoiding his son's eyes.

Oh. "They didn't answer," said Putnam, "because you never asked them. That's it, isn't it?"

The Raft King didn't answer. His jaw twitched. Then he said, "Things are complicated, son. Sometimes it's better not to ask questions."

Suddenly Putnam understood. "You didn't *ask* them. But the fish *told* you anyway, didn't they?" He could hear venom dripping from his voice, and he didn't care. "They told you the sea was dying. They told you to do something to fix it. *Didn't they?*"

"Son—"

"Did you even ask them for help? For more details so you could fix things?"

"They said it was something terrible! In the deep south! The ice! We can't fix that!" The old man took a deep breath. "I'm sure, given time, things can mend themselves." But there was a note of pleading in his voice. "Our country is doing fine right now. We should . . . just keep going as we are. Don't rock the boat."

It was like a punch to the gut. His dad *was* the do-nothing politician he seemed to be. Putnam hadn't wanted to believe it. "How can you be king and not fix things?" He felt his fists curling and uncurling on their own. "You are a terrible king," he said.

His father's head snapped back as if Putnam had punched him, too. Then he took a deep, long breath, almost a sigh. "Show respect, young man."

Putnam glared.

Carefully, slowly, the Raft King unclasped the red cloak and hung it on a hook. Sitting on a brightly embroidered bench beneath the tapestry of Raftworld visiting Tathenn, he leaned forward, elbows on knees. "We might . . . discuss . . . issues in private, but you will not disagree publicly with me at the Session. We present a united front. Remember that tomorrow. Or don't come to the meeting."

"Even if I'm right?"

"Your job is to listen and to learn, not to speak publicly against the king."

"Then I won't be at the Session." Wishing he had a door to slam, Putnam yanked the tent flap aside and left.

His father, cautious as always, didn't follow or call after him.

As PUTNAM walked back through the party, he thought about his future life. He'd be king someday; would he turn out like his dad? His dad, who had been well past middle age when Putnam had been born, who'd never been the kind of dad to take his son fishing or go swimming with him, who by the time Putnam was ten was already bent with arthritis. Who was so old and boring that even his wife—Putnam's adopted mom— couldn't be convinced to stay.

And that was his dad's fault, too. At least partly.

"You okay, Putnam?"

"What?"

"Shaking your head like that. A headache? Want to rest in my family's tent?"

It was one of his schoolmates from Raftworld, a boy

named Olu who was always offering him things, inviting him places, losing to him in games. As much as Putnam liked winning, Olu could beat him at most games if he tried; but he didn't. Most of the other kids were like that, too, flattering Putnam and losing to him, but it had started with Olu, who led the way. Olu was naturally athletic, a good speaker, and smart—and when he came in second to Putnam again and again, the other kids imitated him. Putnam didn't know how to make them stop.

"I'm fine," he said, more brusquely than he'd meant to.

"That's great," said Olu, smiling broadly. "Have a great evening!"

Putnam walked on. He found himself wondering—he wasn't sure why—where the bonfire girl had disappeared to. He glanced around as he skirted the fires, but her face never glinted into sight. She must have gone home—or wherever someone so ragged would disappear to.

It was strange. He'd thought the Islanders would take care of their children. She was pretty clearly about his age, twelve, or maybe ten; how could she look so battered and underfed? And that was just in firelit glimpses. Surely she wasn't so uncared for; she must have torn her clothes and avoided her parents when it was time to dress for the party. Yes, that was it. She was a troublemaker. Probably the kind of girl who picked fights and deserved her bruises—maybe some of them from jumping off cliffs into the sea, or climbing too-high trees and falling.

His mind darted suddenly to his first mother, who had died giving birth to him; and his adoptive mother, the only mom he'd known, missing now for more than half his life. She'd left when he was five. Disappeared. But *he* hadn't become a troublemaker. He was doing fine. He barely even knew she was gone. In fact, he didn't miss her one bit. After all, she'd left him; why should he miss someone who didn't want to be his mom?

His dad and his dad's advisors had raised him to be clean and obedient and never make mistakes. He'd always tried to be as perfect as possible. Even now, after a full day of meetings and parties, he was wearing a clean shirt and had recently washed his face and combed his tight curls. Well, maybe it was time to be done being perfect. Maybe he *should* be a troublemaker.

This girl, though. She bit at his mind and wouldn't leave—because she was so tattered. Because she stood out. Who was she? And why was she here?

She had simply—flickered out. And no one else seemed to notice. He wished again that that was something *he* could do: run away, disappear. He was a good boat pilot, having lived on the sea all his life, and though he didn't have any magical gifts with water like his father did, he did have twelve years of living on the water, good experience to call on. He could slip away to sea. It would be a relief not to attend the Session with his father, to forget for a while that these meetings would never stop happening, and eventually he'd have to be in charge of them as Raftworld's king. Meetings where no real decisions seemed to be made, where nothing seemed to get done.

And this weeklong party would be the best time to leave. His father wouldn't want to upset people by sending out a search party; he'd just assume Putnam, angry at him, was skipping the Session and hanging out with some friends. It might even take him a day or two to notice that Putnam had gone. After all, Putnam wouldn't make a big scene out of leaving like his mom had. He'd just slip away.

He remembered, right after his second mom had left them— had flown off into the world, never to return—Olu's father in his deep voice asking Putnam's father, "Why didn't you beg her to stay? Or start the engines of Raftworld and chase after her?"

Five-year-old Putnam, standing in the next room, pressed his ear against the wall to hear.

His father's quiet words were almost drowned in the slap-slap of water on the raft's bottom. But Putnam heard. "If she wants to go, who am I to try and stop her? I don't interfere in such things."

"But she is your wife!"

"Even so. It is her choice."

Putnam never asked his father about that conversation. Yes, his mom was her own person, with her own choices. But shouldn't his dad have *tried*? His mom was no longer in this world—that much his dad had told him.

I can't find her. But I can try to fix this problem with the sea.

Then he shook himself. What was he thinking? He couldn't sneak away. He didn't even have a boat. Anyway, running away was not something the king's son would do. It would be just like what his mother had done. Irresponsible. Mean.

But he would come back.

He walked along the shore, away from the crowds. The thin moon winked dimly on the water.

He could see the Island governor's face as she said that the Raft King wasn't going to do anything. Her eyes had glowed with sadness, and her mouth had turned in distaste and judgment. A wash of shame hit him like a wave. He couldn't go back to the Session, not until he'd fixed the sea—and made it clear that he wasn't his father, that he'd get things done.On top of all that, he remembered fear in the young governor's eyes, and he felt that, too. What if they lost the sea? He *had* to do something.

But how? Where to go? And how to get there?

His walk had taken him far down the shore. Although he could hear voices in the distance, the beach here was deserted. The night was quiet, waves lapping gently and an owl hooting in the distance. The sea. Turning to salt.

At that moment, he saw a little one-person-size sailing boat, sitting forlornly on the beach, barely pulled in out of the tide, unwatched—as if asking to be borrowed. And at the exact same moment, the thought popped into his head:. *I'll sail to the deep south. And I'll leave tonight.*

2

RAYEL. ABOUT 100 YEARS EARLIER.

*T*HE FUNERAL was over; Solomon's small body had been wrapped and weighted and lowered into the ocean. The songs had been sung. The eulogies spoken. Everyone had cried, even Rayel's mother.

Rayel sat on the edge of Raftworld, her feet dangling in the water so she could feel close to her little brother just a few moments longer. Her eyes were dry now, even though the wind whipped up little splashes on her dress and her face. Everyone had left or just about left; as they filed out of the dock area where the funeral had been held, several of the musicians and speakers, and a few of Solomon's teachers, paused to place their hand on Rayel's shoulder. She didn't acknowledge them. Couldn't.

He was gone. Rayel focused on breathing—she'd felt like she was gasping ever since Solomon's flu had taken a bad turn and his lungs had clogged and he'd lain in bed struggling for air. She couldn't breathe, either. But somehow she was still alive.

A stone rested on her chest. Heavy.

Behind her, Rayel's mother sniffed. "Time to go, dear." The *dear* was because there were still a few people within hearing.

Rayel didn't move.

"Everyone is gone. It's over. Let's go." Her voice was brisk now. Impatient. "I need—your father and I need—to talk to you. At home."

Rayel looked at her mother. Beautiful as always, she stood tall and straight in her long blue gown, a yellow cloth over her head to show she was mourning. She looked good in yellow. Her neck rose slim and dark from her gown, cut just low enough to draw the eye, and her stomach bulged with the baby that was nearly arrived. She was everything healthy and lovely, except for the expression on her face as her eyes swept over Rayel.

Slowly Rayel pulled her legs out of the water and rose, feeling—as always around her mother—grubby and awkward. She was suddenly aware of how old her braids were. As she stood, her foot caught in the long funeral dress—she usually wore pants—and ripped the hem. Rayel's mother rolled her eyes and turned to walk toward home. Rayel followed.

They lived in the center of Raftworld, so the walk took more than a few minutes as they wound through the little houses and gardens and crossed from one lashed-together raft to another. Raftworld was silent this afternoon, in honor of Solomon's funeral—the son of the king of Raftworld. As Rayel and her mother passed, people in their gardens bowed their heads but didn't speak above hushed voices. Only the chickens were untouched by tragedy; they clucked and scrabbled as always.

Rayel's mind wandered as she trailed behind her mom. Her father wanted to talk to her? The Raft King? He never wanted to talk, just to read his books and watch birds, and, when he couldn't avoid it, meet with his advisors about Raftworld. He had wept at Solomon's bedside and again at his funeral, but then had quietly hurried away. She hadn't thought she'd see him again so soon. What could he want to talk about?

It wasn't . . . ? *No,* he couldn't want to talk to her about being the next king of Raftworld. There was a new baby on the way, after all, and that baby would surely be good enough to be the next king.

Like Solomon had been.

Like she would never be.

It wasn't just that she was awkward and no good at making friends. It was also that she was ugly. Not plain. Ugly.

She'd known ever since she'd first overheard her mother say it, when she was barely old enough to understand what the words meant. Solomon too had been born ugly, like Rayel, with a misshapen lumpy head and mashed features and terrible skin (but without her twisted-in feet). Rayel had been eight. She remembered it vividly. Solomon, newborn and wrapped in a blanket, had been handed to their mother, and Rayel and her father had finally been allowed in the room, but instead of showing joy Rayel's mom had shoved the baby back to the midwife. "*He's* ugly, too. I can't take this again. Not again." Her mother had started crying. "Why me?"

The midwife put the baby, who was whimpering, in a cradle and turned to Rayel's father. "This sometimes happens with mamas," she said apologetically. "After-baby sickness. I have some herbs that will make her more content."

The Raft King nodded gravely, as if after-baby sickness were all it was. But Rayel knew better—she knew it then, and she knew it now. There was something bigger wrong with her mother, something that herbs couldn't fix.

While her father and the midwife comforted her mother, Rayel had crept to the cradle and picked up the baby, supporting his head carefully as she'd seen grown-ups do. She sat cross-legged on the floor and curled her whole body around him, her face to his. His eyes, dark brown like hers, stared back at her unblinking. His pale acned face would darken soon, and maybe clear up, too. Definitely he'd look better then. But she didn't care. He was now, already, the most beautiful creature she'd ever seen.

"Don't worry," she whispered. "I'll love you."

And she did, for the next six years. Slowly, his head rounded out and his features smoothed and his skin cleared up. By the time he was toddling, he looked like any normal baby—which is to say, beautiful and messy with drool at the same time. By four years old, he was so full of light and energy and so quick to smile that strangers would stop Rayel to tell her that he was the cutest child they'd ever seen.

By the time he was six, Rayel's mother wanted to be seen with him, to have him follow her around, to have him run to her each day and tell her secrets and draw pictures for her. But instead he did all these things with Rayel—the person who'd fed him, changed him, rocked him to sleep, taken him for walks, read to him, sung to him, and given herself to him for six years. Solomon had many friends; everyone liked him and wanted to be around him. But he loved Rayel most of all.

And Rayel had only one friend, only one person she spoke freely with, only one person who thought she was beautiful and funny and smart and kind and interesting. Solomon.

And this, Rayel thought, watching her mom swishing ahead of her toward home, *is why our mother disliked Solomon. And it is one of the reasons she hates me. Because I got the love that was supposed to be hers.*

At that moment, Rayel's mother turned and gestured to her

to hurry. "If I can walk at a normal pace with a baby inside me, I think you can *try* to keep up."

But when Rayel jogged to walk alongside her, her mom said, "You don't need to hover. Just keep up. Behind me."

She fell back again, but not too far.

When they finally reached the house, their housekeeper—it was a big house, being the king's residence and the place where most government meetings were held—opened the door and said, "Dinner—"

"You may leave now," said Rayel's mother. "We want some time alone, as a family."

The housekeeper nodded sharply, her lips tight. She had loved Solomon, too. Rayel put her hand on the woman's shoulder as she walked into the house and the housekeeper walked out.

Rayel's father sat in the study as always. And suddenly it felt weirdly like a normal day, except that Solomon wasn't there. Rayel tried to pretend, just for a few minutes as her parents murmured to each other, that Solomon was playing boats with his friends down at the docks and would be back for dinner. But the heavy rock wouldn't leave her chest.

Her father held an open book full of drawings of plants and birds. He was replying to something his wife had said. "Do we need to do this now?" Even as he asked, he found his bookmark and closed the volume. His head was uncovered already and he was back in his usual pants and shirt, his dress robe hanging on a hook behind his desk. Rayel's father had a well-trimmed dark beard, but the hair on his head had long since departed. In the dim study, his bald pate glimmered in the lamplight so that he looked like he wore a glowing crown. Whenever she pictured her father in her mind, this is what Rayel saw: night after night, a man alone in his study with a crown of light on his head. Day after day, a bright head turned away toward the horizon and the sky.

Rayel's mother eased herself into a comfortable chair and propped up her feet, sighing. "This child better come soon," she said conversationally. Her stomach rippled with movement as if the baby were agreeing. "And yes, we do need to do it now."

Both parents turned to look expectantly at Rayel, like they thought she was going to speak. But she didn't know what she was supposed to say. And she didn't like being stared at; usually people ignored her, usually she sat quietly in a corner, except when Solomon—

"We need to talk," said her mother. "Your father has some exciting news for you."

Rayel stood in the middle of the room, waiting.

The Raft King crossed and recrossed his feet, reached for his book and then stopped, as if realizing the book wouldn't help him now. "You are growing up," he said.

"Oh, for the sake of the sky and all the heavens," said

Rayel's mother. "We've arranged your marriage. It'll happen next week."

"My what?" She must have heard wrong. Not that marriages weren't arranged; the best ones were—agreed upon by the parents and the child, the spouse chosen carefully with personalities and histories and values and ambitions in mind. But that a marriage had been arranged for her—without her interest and consent, and with her almost a decade younger than when people usually got married. She couldn't have heard right.

Her dad cleared his throat. "Your mother said you wanted—"

"You want to be married," said her mother. As if she'd *ever* said such a thing. "And you want this wedding to happen right away."

"Who . . . ," said Rayel. She couldn't figure out how to finish the sentence. This wasn't the way marriages were supposed to be arranged.

"Well, Cathuu, of course." Her father, smiling, sounded surprised that she didn't know. "Exactly who your mother says you want to marry." He shook his head at her. "I can't believe you didn't guess."

"Must be the stress of the day," said her mother.

"I don't . . . understand," said Rayel.

"Marriage!" said her mother, with a light bell of a laugh. "Sweetheart, rub my swollen feet."

The Raft King scooted his chair closer to his wife's footstool and massaged gently. "Are you feeling okay?"

"This baby is jittery today," said Rayel's mother. But she sounded happy.

How could she be happy, with Solomon dead? How could anyone be happy again?

"I don't want to get married," Rayel said.

Both parents looked up in surprise, as if they'd forgotten she was there.

"I'm . . . too young."

"Ray-*elle*," said her mother.

Rayel was in trouble. She could tell by the emphasis.

Rayel's mother leaned back in her chair to look up at her daughter. "You should be happy that someone so handsome and charming and talented wants to marry someone like you."

"He's twice my age!"

"He's your father's smartest advisor. And he's interested in you. *You*, of all people. I mean, he could have just about anyone." Her eyes raked down Rayel's body and back up again. "Cathuu wants to marry right away."

"No use waiting if you're both in love," said Rayel's father. He sounded like he actually believed what he was saying. Why would her mother have told him that? And why would Cathuu have agreed? Surely her father must have spoken to Cathuu about the marriage—a man who had never shown any interest in Rayel at all, ever. A man whose glance had always darted away from her as if she pained his eyes.

"This will be a good union for the country," Rayel's mother said. She reached for a bottle of lotion and handed it to her husband, who uncorked it and rubbed it into her heels and arches. "Cathuu is a good manager, invaluable to your father. Someday he'll help the next king rule, too. That kind of continuity is good for the country."

Rayel's mother's voice turned serious, her hand resting on her belly. "There is something else, Rayel. Something that is a little more painful to say, but you might as well hear it and grow from it. You did not behave . . . appropriately . . . with Solomon. You tried to turn him into your pet, your shadow. In truth," she said as Rayel gaped at her, "you tried to steal his love from me. From his mother. It didn't work, you know." She was sniffing now, her eyes welling with unshed tears. "But I won't let you do that with this new baby. You need to get into your own house, with your own husband. And you need to do it right away, before this baby is born."

And then Rayel understood the real reason her mother was sending her away: so that the new baby couldn't reach for her the way Solomon did. Couldn't love her.

She'd never *asked* Solomon to love her best of all. She simply loved him with her whole heart, and he loved her back.

"So," said the Raft King. "The wedding will be next week.

Aren't you excited? Something to take your mind off . . . all the tragedy lately."

"It'll have to be a quiet ceremony," said Rayel's mother. "With the country still in mourning—and me so pregnant. A small wedding. You'll wear red." Red was a favorite of Rayel's mother, as it brought out the bright tones in her skin. "And we'll twist your hair up and around your head, like a crown." That was a good look on Rayel's mother, with her perfectly formed head and long neck.

Rayel turned and left the room.

As she walked down the hall to her bedroom, she could hear them talking. "You said she wanted to get married," her dad said.

"Too many emotions today," said her mother. "She's thrilled—or she will be when she thinks about it. It's a far better match than she has a right to hope for."

LATER THAT NIGHT Rayel stood outside Cathuu's house. She'd walked clear across Raftworld in the dark, scooting into quiet gardens when she heard anyone approaching. She didn't want to be seen spying on her fiancé.

But she needed to spy. What in the world was going on? Why would Cathuu be interested in her?

The light was on inside Cathuu's house. His front window, covered with a bright orange curtain, glowed like a fire. On the path outside the garden, Rayel lifted the latch—her fiancé was one of the few people on Raftworld with a gate that closed and latched—and stepped quietly inside, clapping her hand over the bells that were set to ring upon the gate being opened.

Her *fiancé*. What a strange word. What a strange idea. If it weren't so hideous, it would be funny.

She considered knocking at his door and asking him why he wanted to marry her when he couldn't even look at her. But when she neared the front door, she heard voices. Two men talking and laughing. She heard her name. *Rayel.*

She froze and listened.

The words floated out the orange window. Cathuu was talking to another man—she couldn't tell whom.

Cathuu said, "Yes, I really *do* plan to marry her. In all her . . . beauty." Both men laughed. Cathuu had a rich baritone voice, and on the curtain Rayel could see his shadow moving across the room. He was built more like a rower than a politician, but that was part of what people liked about him: his look of belonging to Raftworld. Powerful. The shadow on the curtain outlined his broad shoulders and thick neck, his head wide and flattened a little on top, like he'd battered things down with it. She could not see his face but she knew it well: the straight white teeth, the ready grin, the chiseled features.

She did not like him.

He'd never been kind to Solomon. Or to her.

"Congratulations, then," the other man said. There was a pause while their shadows shook hands. "May I ask why?"

Cathuu laughed. "Do you have to ask?"

"She's not next in line. I mean, technically she is, but the king had already named Solomon to succeed—and now, surely, he'll name the next child. The king and—especially—his wife have always made it clear that Rayel isn't meant to rule. They've never prepared her in any way."

Rayel's fiancé grunted. "True. But the Raft King is sickly, and has been for a long time. If he dies soon, the throne won't go to a baby. Not when there's a perfectly good son-in-law with all the correct experience—and the popularity—to step in and take charge."

"I see," said the other man. And it sounded like he did see. Rayel did, too.

"My wife would be next in line. And—since she's so slow and . . . so unlike a leader—that means I'd be in charge. I mean, does she have the looks to be a king? And the personality?"

The other man laughed. "Does our own king have the personality? He should have been a bird-watcher."

"Even so, he is king."

"True. I see your point, though: *she* can't be king. But—what if the king doesn't die?"

"I think he will."

There was a long pause. Long.

Then the other man laughed again. "Do you mean . . . ?" He sounded admiring.

"I *simply* mean he's a sick old man. Who knows what illness might befall him?" A slight pause now, and then a cheery poof of air, as if her fiancé was blowing out his lips. His shadow shrugged. "If he lives—well, then I'm still his advisor. Nothing lost." Rayel could *hear* her fiancé's grin; it infected his voice with a thick stickiness, like old honey. "When I marry the daughter, my position is secure forever. Advisor for life. Or king. Now, let's talk business."

The men's discussion turned to other things—houses being added on one end of the raft—and Rayel backed slowly away from the window, turning at the end of the garden to slide the latch carefully upward and slip out of the yard unheard.

She was not shocked to hear herself described as *not a leader*—she knew that was what many people thought of her. It was obvious to her—had been, all her life—that ugly people were seen as stupid, untalented. She'd become very good, in response, at hiding her thoughts from people and keeping her face blank in public. Let them think what they wanted. Solomon knew the truth.

Nor was she shocked to hear that her fiancé wasn't in love with her; that was what she'd gone to his house to find out, after all. And it was almost a relief to hear a logical reason for why he wanted to marry her: so that he could keep the power he had now—and maybe even get more power. Rayel reflected that if *she* had power, she might want to keep it, too. She could hardly blame him for that.

No, what shocked her was the fact that her fiancé had called her father sickly. He *wasn't* sickly. Her father had never even had a cold that she could remember, not in her entire life. And that long pause. The *Do you mean . . . ?* from Cathuu's companion.

Her father spent most of his time on the edge of Raftworld, watching birds, or at home with his books, content to let Cathuu attend his meetings and inspect the raft and take charge of public appearances. What if his advisor took advantage of that fact to suggest the king was sick? What if he then *made* the king sick?

Cathuu was, at the least, hoping for the king's death. But what it really sounded like was that he was plotting it.

If he was married to Rayel, and the king suddenly died, it would probably mean that Cathuu would become the next king.

3

ARTIE, 1949. THE PRESENT AGAIN.

*A*RTIE SQUINTED to see the musicians, but didn't move closer, staying just outside the light of the bonfire. She had been listening to music off and on for two days and nights— mostly nights. *Listening* might be too weak a word: she'd been *inhaling* music, breathing it in and living on it. She'd meant to leave the Island right away, as soon as she got north and nicked a boat—to sail off and never be seen or heard from again—but the music had grabbed her and wouldn't let her go.

It wasn't so much the Island songs, though she loved those. Even here in the northern capital, the tunes weren't that much different from what she'd grown up with in the south. A little faster tempo, and maybe a little sharper-toned. But familiar.

No, it was the Raftworld music that hooked her and pulled her in, warm and rich and multilayered, sung to a double-stringed guitar she'd never seen before, often with soft hand-drums that sounded like light waves slapping against the bottom of a boat. Island music was usually danceable; Raftworld music, on the other hand, made her want to sway. She wondered what the guitar would feel like in her hands and how it might sweeten as she strummed it and got to know it.

She was careful, always, not to be seen. She hid in the shadows, not wanting to be noticed or remembered. In spite of the warm weather, Artie wore all her clothing: her leggings and tunic, her luck pouch, her warm jacket, even her ratty arm-warmers. She didn't own shoes, or she would have worn them, too. Carrying everything she owned on her back—and her jackknife in her pocket—saved her having to find a storage spot to hide her things in. It also meant that her scarred arms and shoulders were covered. Her face she couldn't help; the bruise, tender on her cheek, was probably noticeable, but only if someone actually *looked* at her, and no one did.

She'd hiked north into the most important party in the past decade: Raftworld had arrived to the Islands, and for a week or more, the trading and festivities would continue. For Artie, the timing of the Raftworld visit felt almost magical.

Things had been bad at home for a long time now. Artie's mother, when she was alive, protected Artie from her stepdad when he got mad—sending her out to play or fish or *just go away for a while*. Sometimes Artie's mom could get her husband to calm down. Sometimes that didn't work, and he would hit her. Artie could tell when she got back from wherever she'd been sent to, and her mom had bruises from "falling down" or "bumping into something."

When Artie's mom died—after a short but brutal illness, coughing and weak in her bed—Artie's stepdad got worse. Or maybe it was just that now all his anger was aimed at Artie, and she had no one to protect her. She didn't go to school—he said it was too long a walk—and he kept her away from kids her age and from other adults, except when he was around. He controlled everything. If she burned supper, or lost a fish from the net while pulling it in—or even if she hadn't done anything wrong, but he'd just had a bad day—his fists came out, or his open hand for a slap.

There was no reason to stay. As her stepfather reminded her when no one else was around, she was just a lodger now. Not his real kid, and not someone he'd asked to raise. She came up with a plan the week her mom died: when she was a little more grown, she'd build her own cabin at the other end of the village and live on her own.

But over time, it became clear to her that the other side of the village wasn't far enough away. And three nights ago, her life had shifted again. Her stepfather had gone to a bonfire with friends—fellow fishermen—and had come home staggering and muttering. And he'd lurched into the house and *hadn't* hit her—

She shook herself violently and took a deep, slow breath. She wasn't going to think about it—about *him*—anymore. That night, after he had fallen to the floor in a deep, disheveled sleep, she had put on all her clothes, stolen a small knife and a little food, and escaped. She was never, ever going to go back. She'd live by herself starting now. A little cabin far away.

That night she started walking. Her stepfather might try to follow her, but he wouldn't find her. She'd make sure of that. First: north, to the big city, where it would be easy to hide. Then she'd figure the rest out.

And she'd stayed hidden, easily, for the whole first day after she reached Baytown. She finished her stolen food, and she sat in the woods outside town and thought. What was her plan now? Where could she go where she'd never be bothered?

Raftworld arrived that day, and the party started: trading of goods and stories and news. And songs.

The music carried into the forest.

Oh, the songs. That first night after she arrived, when people started singing, she couldn't—she just *couldn't*—stay away. She had to see as well as hear—and she had to hear clearly. She had to know how they created that music. She knew all the Island ballads and, in private, sometimes made up songs and sang them to herself, but she'd never heard any like these Raftworld songs. The scale was even different.

Lurking outside the firelight, she listened for two nights to everything she could. Some songs she heard several times, wandering from place to place and finding different musicians singing different versions. Others she heard only once. All of them were magical, and many she memorized—or at least she memorized fragments, storing them for later, when she might pull them out and play with them.

All the time she wandered and listened, however, she worried about getting caught. She kept scanning the crowds to see if anyone from home was there, hoping that word wouldn't get back about where she was. Everyone liked her stepdad, who was loud and funny. They wouldn't believe her. She'd run away twice before, to other village families, and both times they'd returned her to her joking, beaming stepfather, the nice man who raised his dead wife's troubled and ungrateful daughter. Tathenn wasn't big enough to hide her. She'd sail away and find her own island—something small just for her.

The songs kept pulling her out of her memories and into the present. So many of them were new to her. Wandering through the bonfire parties, she felt almost as if she were stealing music to keep herself alive on her journey. And for wherever she settled at the end of her journey. She'd want these songs later.

The second night, knowing she was going to leave the Islands, she stole real items, too—in the deep dark after the singing ended and everyone drifted to sleep. Only a few things: a rope that someone had left lying out, and a small net resting lonely on the beach. And a bowl someone had set aside for washup later. (She hid that in the hollow of a tree, to retrieve when she was ready to go.) She refused to steal anything she didn't need—not even when she saw a guitar sitting completely unattended outside a tent. She told herself *no* and moved on, though her heart hurt to leave it there. She found a straight stick that looked good for carving—surely she'd have time while at sea—and put it in her pocket with her knife, promising herself she'd whittle something musical. The stick sang back to her from her pocket: *a flute, please,* and she slipped her hand into her jacket and patted the warm wood. Artie's mom had taught her to play flute when she was little, though her hand-carved instrument had been smashed long ago.

Artie stole food, too, but she didn't manage to save any: she ate it as soon as she took it. Since there were tables of party treats just sitting around unwatched, it hardly even counted as stealing. Artie wanted to take some food with her on the boat, but everything sitting out was fresh, with a short shelf life—and each night the leftovers were put away. Besides, she'd lived all her life on food from the sea. Food was easy, and water, too. The sea gave these.

The third night, her last, she stood outside the circle of the central bonfire. The Raftworld storyteller had been singing, accompanied by guitar and drum, and now was beginning to tell a story.

Artie was only half listening, letting the storyteller's voice wash over her as he slid from singing to talking. Something about mangoes.

This story could be a song. She could hear the music in her head, feel it in her throat, twitching to come out. Artie wavered, almost ready to step into the light and share it—in fact, she had thrust her head forward and felt the heat and light in her eyes before she remembered herself and jerked back into the shadows. She needed to stay out of sight. She could sing to herself later.

She clenched her fists and moved about the circle. *Tonight!* She was ready. The weather was perfectly clear and the moon was small, a sliver of a baby's clipped fingernail in the sky. She would leave as soon as the storytelling was over.

A boy about her age, on the other side of the bonfire, frowned. He was a Raftworlder, tall and thin and curly headed, slouching a little with the easy grace of the well loved. It almost seemed as if he were seeing her. *Studying* her. Artie backed up and froze. Why would he be staring at her? But he didn't move or react; he wasn't watching her, after all. No, he was listening to the story, frowning importantly.

Even without his Very High Class expression on his face, Artie could tell he was rich. His clothing alone was probably worth more than her stepfather made in a year of fishing and trading. And when the boy started walking again, slowly moving around the circle, people parted and moved out of his way like he was a boat sailing through water.

He was probably a pampered baby who'd always gotten whatever he wanted. No, that was unfair. He didn't have the sneer of a spoiled brat—but he did have the air of someone who had no idea how easy his life was. She'd seen that before, even in the south, where life was grittier than up here in the city where all the rich folks and rulers lived.

Eventually the singing started again, and she forgot the boy and wilted into the sound, joyful and sad at the same time, of the old stories being sung. Or maybe it was just that she felt the joy of listening mixed with the sadness of being unable to join in. The joy of eating along with the knowing, deep in her gut, that she'd never be full. She felt half-this, half-that. Like she was here but not here, listening and sneaking food all while remaining invisible to everyone around her—because they were all paying attention to their own lives and because she was so good at disappearing.

The music stopped; the party was beginning to break up.

She didn't want to leave yet.

It had to happen tonight. No one would even notice a boat gone until morning. She'd climb aboard a little rig pulled up on the shore and she'd sleep for a couple of hours, after which she'd leave, when the world had gone dark and people were finally sleeping. Then she'd have several good hours to find a current and get miles and miles away.

She didn't know much about sailing long distances—okay,

she didn't know *anything* about sailing long distances—but she had two things going for her. She knew small boats from all her years on the coast, and she'd always been a hardy sailor on her stepfather's fishing boat. How tricky could it be to sail far out to sea?

She crawled aboard the smallest, farthest-away-from-all-the-crowds vessel she could find and huddled in its tiny cabin, waiting for the sky to completely darken and the crowds to die down. The night had gotten cool. She wrapped her thin arms around her body and rubbed her ribs, trying to stay warm and also trying not to rub too hard on the bruises. Her stomach growled, loudly. She was so hungry. And so tired.

And so, so ready to be gone.

4

PUTNAM. THE PRESENT.

*P*UTNAM LEFT the shore and the little boat he'd seen there, thinking over his astonishing plan as he walked back to the tent. He could leave. He could sail away—south—and investigate the problem of the salt in the sea, and come back with information. With proof. Proof that his dad was wrong: too slow to act, too scared to *do* something to fix a problem.

He slipped home through the crowds and the singing and the storytelling to an empty tent. Putnam's anger rose again. His dad must be at one of the bonfires, making his nightly rounds with the people. The Raft King prided himself on listening to his people. *But,* Putnam thought, *listening isn't the same as doing . . .*

He, Putnam, was going to *do*. And he'd come back a hero, as someone who'd solved the problem of the bad water. He'd be a different kind of person—and someday a different and better kind of king—than his father. Not someone who stood by and let his son's mother run off. Not someone who sat by while the sea turned to salt.

He packed a change of clothes—warm, wet-weather clothes—and some dried food and a few empty water sacks to fill with seawater when he got to shore. It was crazy to carry water with you when you traveled *on water*, but he didn't know how brackish the sea would get before he reached the source of the problem. It was possible that it would become undrinkable.

Putnam slid out of the tent quietly. He didn't leave a note. His dad probably wouldn't miss him tomorrow; when the Session meeting started in the morning, his dad would simply think he was skipping it in a sulk, still angry about their argument. And when his dad didn't see him at night, he'd just think he was sleeping in a different tent with other kids. After all, Olu had invited him to a big sleepover only the day before. His dad probably wouldn't even realize he was missing for a couple of days. And by then he'd be long gone.

Putnam, his sack of supplies over his shoulder, stopped walking so suddenly that someone stumbled around him, muttering. He was about to do exactly what his adoptive mom had done when she'd left without explanation when he was five. There one day, and the next day gone. He'd seen her take off, and he'd thought for years that she might come back, but she never did.

And his dad had shrugged and let her go.

She didn't even leave a note.

He couldn't be like that, not even if his dad deserved it. He had to leave a note, so that when his dad *did* notice he was gone, at least he'd know where his only child had disappeared to.

And unlike his mom, Putnam would come back. He would.

Hastily, he returned home, jotted a couple of sentences, and thrust the note under the pillow. There it would stay, safely undiscovered until the king got worried and searched his room. Putnam would have enough time to escape—and yet the note would help his dad not to worry too much.

Although his dad would worry a little, of course. That couldn't be helped. But it was the king's own fault. If he'd agreed to do something about the bad water, Putnam wouldn't have had to step forward. Really, he was saving the old man from embarrassment. Besides, his dad had said to stay out of the Session. Maybe he deserved a little worry.

PUTNAM SNUCK BACK to the beach and stuffed his pack into the bushes, returned to the crowds, and joined a campfire until the partying died down and the moon set and the beach cleared. Then he retrieved his pack. On the beach, poking out from under a small pile of rocks, he left money to pay for the little boat he'd chosen; he wasn't a thief. He crept across the dark sand and climbed into the boat. It was perfect: small enough for one person to handle, and in the center a snug cabin with a latching door in which he could store things and stay warm. He peeked in the cabin's window—there were some tarps piled in the corner and a small heater in the middle.

Pausing only long enough to lean his bag inside the cabin, Putnam rowed silently out to sea, loosening the sail when he was sure he'd gotten far enough from shore and it wouldn't be spotted. He circled the big Island and headed south.

South was new territory for him. Even though Raftworld traveled constantly, they never went much farther south than the southern tip of the big Island of Tathenn that the Colay people lived on, because the water and weather quickly turned cold— and Raftworld was a warm-weather country. So Putnam wasn't familiar with what might lie in this direction. But the fish had said the problem was in the deep south, so that was where he would go.

He didn't know more than that: head south. But he was hopeful that things would become clearer once he got there. Wherever *there* was.

As morning dawned, he was well out of sight of the Islands. Best of all, he'd found a narrow current that was carrying him almost directly southward, and he'd gratefully taken down the sail—which he found hard to use anyway, as modern

Raftworlders favored hydraulics—and simply rode the current, the sun shining on his face and the light breeze making the world seem brand-new. Everything was perfect. In the light of this calm blue morning, his journey felt like destiny. He stretched his legs out, pulled the food bag out of the cabin, and removed a loaf of bread, along with some plums, the only food he'd packed that wasn't dried.

As he broke the loaf open and dipped his nose to smell the rich yeastiness of Island bread, a noise behind him broke the silence. Not an expected noise. Not a birdcall, not waves splashing lightly against the boat's side, not the creaking of the boat itself.

A human voice. Angry.

"Get off my boat!" said the voice, high-pitched and half strangled, the way a ghost might sound. "Or I'll *kill* you."

5

RAYEL. ABOUT 100 YEARS EARLIER.

RAYEL STOOD on the path outside her fiancé's fenced garden, frozen for a moment in the thought that he wanted her father dead and equally frozen in the uncertainty about what to do. Her mother, if Rayel told her what she'd overheard, would likely say Rayel was making up stories to avoid marriage. Her father was too interested in his books and birds and in believing his wife to take his daughter seriously. There was no one to whom she could turn.

She rubbed her head in frustration and confusion, then tapped its largest bump, off to the side of her head—the one that made her look particularly lopsided. Usually tapping helped her think. This time it did not; it only reminded her of how ugly she was. How could her father possibly believe that Cathuu wanted to marry her?

Then the light dimmed inside the house, and she knew that

whoever was in there would be coming out soon. It wouldn't do to be caught eavesdropping after such a conversation. She squared her shoulders and jogged down the path, taking care to be quiet while she hurried.

She didn't go home. Her feet took her to the docks almost without her even having to think. It was like they knew where to go.

Her brain knew, too. A year or so ago, when she was thirteen, she and Solomon had almost run away. They'd gotten as far as the docks and then she'd backed out, scared of the unknown—and scared to bring Solomon into it. She'd thought he was better off on Raftworld.

She shoved the memory down. Now she knew better. She had to leave, as soon as possible, in one of the little boats. In less than a week she'd be married. She needed to leave before that happened. If she didn't marry Cathuu, he would have no reason to kill her father: he wouldn't be next in line for the throne, being no blood relation at all to Rayel's family.

Somehow that thought made up her mind. She didn't know how else to work against this awful man, but by leaving, she'd foil all his plans. She'd win.

Not right this minute, though. She needed her own plan— or at least some supplies.

Okay. She'd leave tomorrow. One day to pack and say good-bye to Raftworld. There was no one here she'd miss now that Solomon was gone, but she'd miss the world itself—the chickens and the small birds, the lush gardens, the water slapping lightly on the bottom of the raft day and night. The feeling of movement under your feet all the time, as if you were part of the world's breathing—something no one on land ever really got to experience.

Well, she'd still be on a boat. It would be okay.

She just needed to figure out where to go—and for how long.

She'd leave tomorrow night.

THE NEXT DAY, late in the morning, Cathuu came over to have lunch with his fiancé—which is to say, *her*—and she called from her bed that she was too sick to get up.

Her mother came to the room and stood in the doorway, peering into her dim room. "Get up right now, young lady. Don't embarrass me."

"I don't feel good at all." Rayel coughed. "I think I might throw up."

"Well." Her mother's voice sounded like she didn't believe her. "You can stay in bed today, without any food. I mean, you wouldn't want to eat if you feel like you're going to throw up."

Ugh. Rayel was hungry, too.

"And you can't hide from him forever. You'll come to like him when you're married. He's a very handsome man. And he's really going somewhere."

Sure. He'll be king if he has his way.

Rayel's mother shut the door firmly and returned to the dining room. Rayel could hear her tinkling laugh mixing with Cathuu's booming tones. Their voices rang through most of the afternoon.

By evening Rayel was famished. She packed a few useful items—a change of clothes, a spool of string, a small scissors—but truly she didn't have much in her bedroom that would be good for living on a small boat.

And for how long? She thought she'd try for at least a year. Maybe in a year she could return—maybe sneak back in the night—and see if Cathuu had married someone else meanwhile. He probably would. He was already nearly thirty years old. And if he were married to someone else, it would be safe to return, probably.

It irked her to think that she was saving her dad's life and he'd never know about it. He'd keep trusting Cathuu. She considered writing a note of explanation and leaving it on his desk . . . but knowing her father, he'd show it to his wife, and she'd say Rayel was lying, reaching pathetically for attention.

That night when the housekeeper had gone and her parents were in bed, she snuck out of her room with her bag, ate the leftovers in the kitchen, and packed up dried goods for her trip. In the garden shed she took a fishing net, a pot and a bucket, a knife, and a few more items she thought she'd need.

And then she escaped.

She slid a small boat into the water and rowed and eventually raised the sail and headed away, not even sure where she was headed. Maybe to the Islands. There were other people there. Or maybe someplace with no people, to bide her time until she might return.

To begin with (and because Raftworld never traveled far in that direction), she headed south. No one would look for her there. South was a place where she could disappear.

6

SHE MUST have been hidden in the pile of tarps in the boat's cabin, and now she stood just outside the cabin, screaming that she was going to kill Putnam.

It was that girl. The one who had hovered around the fire, looking so abandoned and poor and bruised. And *what* did she just say? Did she really just threaten to kill him? She looked like she could barely stand.

The girl swayed, fists clenched. "Do you not speak English? Get off my boat. Or else."

"I speak English," Putnam said. "Better than you." Her Islander accent was strong; probably Colay was her better language. "What are you doing here?"

"You're on *my* boat." She grabbed an oar and jabbed it at him. "Get off. And don't get any closer."

He put his hands in the air, partly to block the oar and

partly to show her that he wasn't going to grab a weapon as she had done. Scrawny kid. She was so small, he wondered if she was even younger than he'd thought at the bonfire. But her face looked older, so maybe she was his age after all. She definitely didn't recognize him as the king's son, or she wouldn't talk like this.

It was surprising that she hadn't seen him standing next to his father at various meetings and dinners. But then, she probably hadn't been at those fancy events.

"How old are you, anyway?" he said. It wasn't what he meant to ask.

"Twelve. Now *go*."

"Are you lost?"

She almost shrieked. "GET. OFF." She jabbed again, stumbled, and caught herself. The oar was too heavy for her sticklike arms. She looked half starved.

He backed up a couple of steps, out of range of the oar, and tried to speak gently. "We're way out at sea. I *can't* get off the boat. Let's sit and talk. Just talk."

She glared, then nodded stiffly, the oar clattering to the boat's floorboards. But she didn't sit. "Why are you in my boat?"

"Well, I didn't know it was your boat. Does it—" There was no way to ask politely. "Does the boat *belong* to you?" No way did this ragged urchin own a boat. "Or maybe it's your parents' boat. Where are they?"

"It's mine," she said sharply. "I stole it all by myself. You go steal someone else's boat."

He laughed; he couldn't help it. "You know if you stole it, you don't own it, right? It's not actually yours."

"I stole it fair and square. Besides, what are *you* doing but trying to *re*-steal it? That's worse than stealing. I was only stealing from a rich man. You're stealing from a poor little girl."

When she put it that way, it sounded bad, but Putnam reminded himself of the money he'd left behind on the sand—which at the time he'd thought of as his *renting* the boat. Surely renting a boat that someone else had already stolen wasn't as bad as stealing in the first place? His brain felt twisted up.

"So you should go get yourself a different boat," she concluded.

"But I can't. We're already at sea."

"I'm not stupid. I know that." She stood, swaying and thinking. In the growing light, Putnam could see once again the classic Islander look, with lighter brown skin (under the bruises) and straighter hair than his, and an old-fashioned islander luck pouch hanging around her neck from a cord. She looked as if she'd run away wearing all her belongings; underneath, she was all bones and angles. Her face and hands, the only parts of her body not covered with clothing other than her feet, looked—well, the skin on her neck and hands looked strange. Wrinkled like cloth and faded pinkish-white in places. It looked a little like his father's scars from the fire when Putnam was a baby. But her scars looked new and fresh. He realized he was staring and forced himself to look away.

Reluctantly, he said, "I guess I could—take you back to your home . . ." He didn't want to; he wanted to keep going south. But maybe he could sail her back to the southern part of the Island, away from any people, and drop her off at night . . . And then he'd have to convince her to go ashore without the boat she considered herself the owner of. Or he'd have to get another boat, this time without paying for it, since he'd just spent all his ready money. It would be tricky. But he'd be rid of this little kid.

"No," she said. Firmly, as if she were bracing herself for an argument. "Not going back. Where are you headed?"

"Why? You want to come with me?" He imagined himself attacked with oars and glared at for an entire trip.

"You can drop me off somewhere."

"But I'm not going to Raftworld, I'm going *away* from it. And if you want me to take you back to Tathenn—"

"NO."

"But there isn't anywhere else for you to go. Not with people."

She lifted her chin so that it jutted out, and her eyes sparked with determination, even scrawny as she was. "Then take me somewhere without people."

THEY WERE at a standstill—so to speak. The girl refused to go back, and Putnam refused to take her onward. This was *his* adventure, and he wasn't a babysitter. And if he didn't sail her to Tathenn or Raftworld—well, he couldn't just drop her off somewhere uninhabited. (And where, anyway? There were no islands as far as the eye could see.)

But while they argued and glowered, they were in fact moving southward, riding the current Putnam had found.

The girl shouldn't be taking a long ocean trip. While she had probably fished in the shallow waters around her island, Putnam had grown up on the ocean itself and he knew how the water worked: how to find food while traveling, how to read the sky, how to navigate. The girl might know how to sail a small boat, but she was an Islander, which meant that she'd never taken a long voyage—probably never been out of sight of the big Island itself.

She kept glaring.

Finally, Putnam said, "Fine." Giving in was the only option he could see. She'd have to come along—for now. "But I won't leave you somewhere without people, like you said. You can't possibly live by yourself out in the middle of nowhere—"

"Yes I can."

"—and anyway there aren't even any islands out here as far

as I can tell. So you can come with me, and when the trip is over, we head back to Tathenn." A stony look passed over her face, but before she could argue, he said, "If you really don't want to go back to Tathenn, we can figure it out then. You can come to Raftworld with me."

Though she didn't say *yes*, she didn't pick up the oar again, and Putnam decided that was a good enough response for now. "Where were you planning to sail to, anyway?" he said.

She shrugged. "Where are *you* going? And how long of a trip will it be?"

What a difficult question to answer! What could he say? *I'm going south to figure out what's making the water go bad—and to fix it if I can—and the trip will last as long as it takes to do that?* There was no answer that sounded smart, so he decided to pull rank.

"It's a secret mission. I'm the Raft King's son."

She narrowed her eyes but didn't respond.

They sat in silence for a few minutes, Putnam angry . . . at himself. He should be better at talking with subjects. He usually *was* better. He was going to be the next Raft King. But now, with one small world to rule—a tiny boat—and one small subject—a sullen girl—he was failing.

He straightened his shoulders. *No.* He was good at this. He'd get to know this girl, and within a day or two—probably by suppertime tonight—she'd be friendly and loyal. She'd tell him all about herself. She'd like him and want to help him with his mission. She *would*.

He was, to be honest, a little hurt that she hadn't recognized him. But maybe she wasn't good with faces.

Putnam glanced forward, but there was nothing on the southern horizon—only water all around them. "We should start by getting to know each other a little. If we're going to be traveling together." He settled back in the boat. "We've got time."

She crossed her arms.

At that moment, Putnam decided that he would *make* this girl talk. Make her give up her secrets. Because it was obvious she was keeping something to herself, and that she'd run away with no intention of returning—so it had to be something serious that was driving her. And he wanted to know.

He'd start with easy questions, and pretty soon she'd be telling him everything. "So," he said, stretching, "I'm Putnam. What's your name?"

"Putnam? The Raft King's son?" She seemed shocked.

So she'd heard of him. "Yes. But I'm just a normal person. On this boat we're completely equal."

"Not equal. I stole it first."

"Right." He felt like he was losing control of the conversation. "I'm twelve too. What's your name?"

She glared for a moment. Finally she said, "Artie."

"I don't really know how names work on Tathenn. How did you get it?"

"How did you get *your* name?"

He almost sighed. Why couldn't his stowaway be someone friendly? "It's a good story, actually. My mom died when I was born, before she and my dad had agreed on a name for me. And my dad almost died, too. Right after my mom's funeral there was a fire. My aunt had taken me for a walk, so I wasn't on our section of the raft when it burned. My dad was there, napping, and he got burned pretty bad—but he's fine now."

It wasn't that hard for him to tell what happened, because he'd been too young to remember either his first mother or the fire; so both tragedies seemed interesting and awful—but like a story, not like something that had happened to *him*. Not like when his second mother—the one he remembered—left him. *That* he wasn't going to talk about.

His entire home—the whole square of raft—had burned down all from one unwatched candle, and Raftworld itself had narrowly missed a catastrophic fire. The nation had changed their system of cooking since then—no one had a personal cooking fire anymore but went to community kitchens to cook, kitchens with water siphons at each corner and axes to chop this one raft away from the larger raft if ever there were another fire. The blaze after his first mother's death had changed their world. And his father, of course, still carried the scars on his arms and hands. Like this girl.

"Go on," said the girl, and he realized he hadn't been talking, only thinking.

"Oh. All the time that my dad was recovering from his burns, I still didn't have a name. Everyone just called me Junior. But then my adopted mom showed up."

"Showed up?"

"In a storm. She just—showed up on Raftworld. That happens sometimes, you know—even on the Islands."

Artie nodded. She must have heard stories about how sometimes people arrived from the first world. Rare as an arrival was, it was memorable when it happened. Putnam's new mother had been such a person, blown over to their world in a storm.

"And she became good friends with my dad, and when it was time for my naming ceremony, he asked her to name me something hopeful, and she named me Putnam. It's—well, I don't know what it means, exactly." He'd never thought to ask her before she ran off and left them. He'd been too young. "It's just a name from her world."

Artie shrugged. "It's an okay name, even if you don't know what it means. It's probably something good."

"What does your name mean?"

She narrowed her eyes, thinking for a moment, as if

weighing what story to tell. "It's from the first world, too. You know about the big group of immigrants who came to Tathenn a couple hundred years ago?"

Putnam nodded, thinking of the tapestry in his father's tent, the one with the boats of bewildered people from the first world arriving on Tathenn.

"It's a word from their code language. Thief code, actually. Artie is a nickname. Short for Artful Dodger."

He shook his head, confused. Why would she be called *Artful Dodger*?

"I thought you spoke English." For a quick second, her mouth quirked up at one corner, and Putnam thought that might mean she was teasing. "Artful Dodger is the code word for *lodger*. From the first world people. And after—since I'm an orphan, that's what my stepdad started to call me, and then every-one did, as a joke, and it just stuck. Artful Dodger. Because I was camping out in someone else's house. Because I didn't have my own home."

"Okay, but—but that's not the name your mom gave you. Not your birth name."

"No." She glanced down at her hands, with the little round burns dotted across them. "But it's what I've been called for a good year now."

"What did your mom name you?"

There was a long, long pause before she answered, so long that Putnam thought she wasn't going to speak.

Then she said, "Anna. It's an old English name. But that name is gone."

She didn't look him in the eyes, and she spoke in a hard tone, the words like sharp pebbles. This wasn't a good time to contradict her. "Well," he said slowly, "Artie kind of works as a nickname for Anna, too." It really didn't, but he was searching for something nice to say. "So if you ever change your mind and think that Anna fits you again, you won't have to change your nickname. That's smart."

"I'm done talking," the girl said. "I'm going to rest. And if you come over here while I'm sleeping and—and do anything around me, I'll knife you."

"You have a knife?"

She didn't bother answering, just scooted back into the cabin, into the pile of tarps she'd crawled out of, and tucked it around herself like a cocoon. Closed her eyes.

He didn't think she was actually sleeping—there was something too twitchy and watchful about her face. But he decided to pretend she was and have a little time to himself. He leaned carefully over the edge of the boat and scooped up a handful of water. Drank it in, then twisted up his face. Eww. Definitely saltier than it had been at the Islands. Still drinkable, but not tasty.

Deep in thought, he refilled the water sack that he'd emptied earlier in the night and filled the water sacks he'd brought and a little barrel he'd found on the boat, too. Filled everything he could find that would hold water. If the water got much worse, it might not be drinkable.

The sun was high in the sky, and he still hadn't slept. He faced forward, propped his chin in his hands, and watched the southern waters dance ahead of him as the boat traveled. Slowly his eyes closed.

LATER IN the day, after Putnam had dozed in the warm sun for several hours, Artie emerged from the cabin.

Putnam asked, "Hungry?" and when she agreed to split the last of the bread with him, he said, in the most offhand-yet-caring voice he could manage, "Can you tell me why you ran away?"

7

ARTIE. THE PRESENT.

*T*HERE WAS seriously no way that Artie was answering that question. And his too-kind voice didn't fool her. He was digging for information.

He'd already dug too much. She'd even told him her name—her original name that her mother had given her—and simply because he acted friendly when he asked. She wasn't going to fall for that again.

She hunched over her bread, chewing. Good bread. She was so hungry; in the past couple of days, since she'd arrived in the capital, she'd been able to pilfer bits of food from different places, but there would never be enough food in the entire world to satisfy her. Even when her mom was alive, they'd often gone hungry because her mom was too sick to work in the fields. And then they'd met that nice-seeming, funny, loud fisherman from the village near where they'd been staying, and he'd taken an interest in helping them, and he'd eventually married Artie's mom. They'd had enough food for a while. Mostly fish. Fish and, soon, the fisherman's fists. But there *was* food.

But since . . . since her mom had died, she'd felt constant hunger. Not just for her mother. She was hungry for lots of things—things she wasn't going to tell this Putnam boy about. A kid who looked like everything in his life had been handed to him on a delicate fruit plate with a little jewel-encrusted spoon. A kid who probably had all kinds of family and friends to love him and take care of him. Friends who wouldn't return him to his awful stepdad if he tried to leave.

Artie shrugged to herself. No need to get to know him just because he happened to have stolen the same boat she had. She was on her own—finally, miraculously—and she would stay that way.

She ate the entire hunk of bread in silence. Putnam ate, too, slowly. He ate only about half his bread and put the rest back in the waterproof food sack. "We can catch fish for supper," he said, "so don't worry about finishing your bread."

The light was slanting almost sideways now, as the sun approached the western horizon. All the planes on Putnam's face stood out sharply, and his curls glistened. His skin shone; his teeth almost glowed. He was too healthy.

He leaned far over the lip of the boat and washed his

hands and face, whooping a little at how cold the water was. "Wow, that'll wake you up. I think if we decide to bathe or swim, we'll shiver." He dried off his face on his clean shirt. Then he sat and faced her. "I'll start," he said. "I'll tell you why *I'm* out on the ocean."

"I didn't ask."

He looked startled for a brief second, then said, "But maybe you'll find it interesting. And maybe you've heard something that can help me. You're from Tathenn, right? You're not from the south end by any chance, are you?"

She glared. She was not going to let him weasel information out of her so that he could turn the boat around and return her to where she came from.

He shrugged, as if he hadn't really expected an answer. Then he said, "I've been sent to investigate the southern sea and find out what's causing the water to go bad." He paused. "You know the water is turning salty, right? It's worst on the south shore of Tathenn."

She didn't bother to hide her eye-roll. "That's been obvious to everyone on the Islands for a while now. On the south shore we don't even drink ocean water anymore unless we run out of rainwater."

"So you *are* from the south end. Well, it's even worse now. We've been heading south all night. Taste the water."

She narrowed her eyes at him but didn't move. She'd try the water later, when he wasn't hovering around, watching her.

"Anyway, I'm going to figure out what the problem is."

"And then?"

"And then . . ." He ran his hand over his head, shrugging. "Stop it, I guess. Fix it."

"Fix it." What did he think he could do? He was only a kid.

"Yes." Suddenly he jutted out his chin. "If I can't fix it myself, I can at least bring people back to the—the problem, whatever it is, and tell them what's wrong. I'm going to figure it out."

She barely stopped herself from rolling her eyes again—and only because he looked so . . . worried all of a sudden, like he wanted to be a hero but deep down wasn't sure he could be. Like there was a tiny weasel of self-doubt buried inside him somewhere, twisting to get out.

And that made her like him. Just a little.

"So," he said. "Why are *you* running away?" He grinned. "You can tell me. I won't turn you in or anything."

And, Artie told herself, *this is why you don't make friends with people. They are all of them way too prying and then they don't believe you.* There was so much of her story she didn't want to talk about— didn't want to remember. She closed down her face, turned her back on him, and stared north, to where they'd been. She stayed frozen that way until she was sure he knew they were done talking.

THE REST OF THE DAY passed in almost silence, but she couldn't ignore this boy forever—the boat was too small for that, and he was way too friendly and kept talking to her. Being nice. It was weird.

The first night she didn't sleep—she couldn't get beyond a light doze with him nearby, snoring just feet away from her. All night she drifted off, pinched herself awake, and daydreamed, hunched in the corner of the cabin.

The next morning Putnam stretched when he woke, smiling and wrinkling his nose in the light that streamed in the window of the little room. He rubbed his head with his palm, smoothing his tight curls. Then he looked closely at Artie as if studying her, and said, "I think I'm going to sit on the front of the boat for a couple of hours, just . . . catching the breeze and thinking. If you want to sleep longer, you should shut the door to keep out the wind and catch a few more winks. Oh, and you'll probably need to latch the door so it stays shut—you don't want it to slam open while you're sleeping."

She nodded, exhausted, and he rolled up his blanket, stored it neatly in the corner, and left, shutting the door carefully behind him. After she'd locked it, she fell to the floor and dropped into a long sleep that lasted until the sun was streaming into the opposite window. She still felt a little tired—and stiff beyond belief—but knew it was past time to get up.

Putnam sat in the front of the boat, arms wrapped around himself. The breeze was cool, and he'd left his warm clothing in the locked cabin. The food was stored in the cabin, too—he hadn't eaten all day.

But he didn't say any of that. "You're up! It's been a great day so far—it's good that you can catch some of it."

"Sorry."

"What? No—you needed the sleep. Hiking up from the southern part of the island to the capital was probably exhausting." His eyes flicked over to her, then back out to sea. "I figure we can eat dinner and then I'll drop anchor for a bit and we can wash up—I know I need a swim."

Artie suddenly could feel all the sleep and dirt on her body and clothes. Was he trying to say that she stank? That she needed a bath?

Then she shrugged to herself. What did she care what he thought? "You'd be grimy too if you'd traveled so far." Then she stopped, horrified at herself. She hadn't meant to speak out loud.

"Exactly," said Putnam. "And I haven't walked nearly as far as you. I mean, I assume you've walked a long distance. I just stepped out of a tent and onto a boat. I can't believe how tough you are." He said it like he was impressed, not repulsed.

She didn't know how to respond—what did one say to something that sounded like a compliment? "I'll get the food."

"That's great. I was thinking that we'll finish the scrap of bread that's left and then move on to the plums. We have only a couple days' worth of fresh food—but there's plenty more in the ocean." He paused. "I hope."

They swam after dinner, on opposite sides of the boat. Artie was pretty sure Putnam was stripping down and washing clothes while he swam—he brought a smooth stone with him and some seaweed soap they'd found on the boat—but she kept a layer of clothes on, rubbing them with her hands as best she could and hoping they'd come clean in the water. Her skin, still raw and bruised, she avoided scrubbing, merely wiping it gently with an edge of cloth.

After she felt clean, she climbed back on the boat and toweled off as much as she could with a blanket. Then she went back in the cabin, shivering. The water was comfortable, but the bite in the air after leaving the water was suddenly sharp. Inside the cabin she turned on the heater and sat close to it.

"What's that song?" asked Putnam, entering the cabin. The blanket was draped over his shoulders, and he was carrying his wet shirt.

"Nothing," she said. She hadn't even realized she'd been singing.

"Isn't that one of the island songs I heard around the bonfires?"

She shrugged.

"You have a really nice voice."

She shrugged again and looked away. She and her mother used to sing all the time, embroidering the songs they knew and stitching in new words or notes to suit the occasion. Sometimes they made up songs, whole cloth. But since her mom's death, Artie didn't sing. She had at first, but it had irritated her stepfather, especially if the fishing hadn't been good that day, or if he'd had an argument with someone, or if the weather was bothersome, or if he was short of money—or any number of other things that might go wrong. She was never sure when those bad days would be, so she'd stopped singing except when she was sure she was alone.

But here, somehow, she'd forgotten.

"Never mind," Putnam said, and she realized he had probably been waiting for a response from her. He draped his shirt over a hook near the heater and sat down opposite Artie. "It feels good to be clean, doesn't it?" He peered at her. "Your face is bruised."

He waited like he thought she would say something. Confess something.

The room felt like a trap.

The door was behind her. She could leave. She would go sit outside in the cold.

Putnam continued. "The spots on your arms—were you in a

fire?" Then, before she could do anything, while she was frozen in shock that he would mention the scars, he said, "Because my dad has scars, too—from the fire when I was little. After my first mom died."

She sat very still. He wasn't really asking about her. He just wanted to talk about himself. That was okay. That was something she could handle.

"He has an enormous scar on one arm," said Putnam, "not lots of small ones like yours. And when that one healed, it made his arm look wrinkled, like really, really old skin. But he has some little scars on the other arm, like yours, where his arm didn't get burned completely, but ash fell on him, and it made dots. When his arm healed, it looked like someone drew little white dots all over."

She nodded. He could talk about his dad all day as long as he didn't ask her questions.

"Like yours," Putnam said. "They're faded now, but I think they must have looked like yours when they were newer. Dots all over. So is that what happened? A fire?"

She yanked the sleeves down and leaned toward the heater, hunching over her knees. "Hot oil," she said. "From a pot. It splashed on me when it fell." That was mostly true. Her stepdad had thrown the pot. And he had been sorry afterward.

Putnam needed to stop now. She needed him to stop.

"I never realized—I never thought about how my dad's burns must have looked when I was a baby." Putnam leaned toward her to see better, and she shrugged even deeper into her clothing. "Your arms look like stars. Like there's a constellation there." He paused. "How did the pot fall? What happened?"

She stood and went outside, even as she could hear Putnam in the background saying, "Don't go. Artie. I didn't mean to offend you. The burns marks are . . . *pretty*. What I'm trying to say is . . ."

The ocean roared in her ears, like she was an empty shell, and she couldn't hear anything else.

The scars weren't pretty. There was nothing pretty about what had happened. If she let herself, she knew she could still feel the oil splashing on her, and she thought she would feel it all her life.

A few minutes later Putnam stood next to her, his wet head and trousers, warm from the cabin, now steaming in the cold outside air. "Artie. I'm sorry. I promise not to talk about it anymore. In fact, I won't talk at all if you don't want me to. Please come back inside, or you'll catch your death of cold."

The wind bit her. She went back inside and sat down. They sat for a long time, until Artie was almost completely dry.

Finally she said, "*Catch your death of cold*?"

"Something my dad says."

"You sound like an old man."

"I'll try not to say that again."

"It's okay. It's just—do you hang out with other kids? Or only with old people like parents?"

"I'm busy learning how to be the next king," said Putnam. "I mean, I have friends, I get invited to a lot of things, but it's because I'm the next ruler. I don't have a *good* friend, like you could tell everything to . . ." He trailed off, looking embarrassed. "I'll get supper. The plums are a little too ripe, and the water is kind of salty. But I'm hungry enough that it will taste great. I bet you are, too."

She nodded to show that she was hungry, too. Pulling her knees in to her chest, listening to Putnam rummage in the bags behind her, her eyes drifted to her arms. Carefully she pushed up a sleeve and squinted in the dim light. The white scars that dotted her arm did look like stars. They did. She could see it now.

What constellation might they be? She found shapes and traced them with her free hand: A bird pecking for a worm. A small backpack. A flower going to seed. Or maybe the constellation was something mythological: A winged horse rearing up before taking flight. A sea monster stretching its tentacles in all directions. A bear reaching for something up high, maybe honey in a tree. There was so much there, in her arm, stars and planets and galaxies and maybe even entire universes.

"Ready?"

She looked up to see Putnam, still draped in his blanket like it was a king's cape, holding a plate of food.

She shoved the sleeve back down to hide the burns—which is what they were.

No. Not ready.

8

RAYEL. ABOUT 100 YEARS EARLIER.

OURTEEN YEARS old and alone in the world, Rayel stood on the small boat she'd stolen—the first thing she'd ever stolen in her life other than, as her mother claimed, her brother's love—and hoisted up a series of little sails. She was glad that when she was ten she'd insisted on learning how to sail—even though her mother had said she'd never need the skill. She lived on a giant raft—how could she not need such a skill someday? Even back then, she'd known when to listen and when not to listen to her mother. Mostly: not.

The boat tacked steadily south. When she needed to sleep, she pulled in the sails, dropped anchor, and curled up in the little covered portion of the boat, which was just big enough—and well sealed enough—for a thin, dry mattress and a small pantry of food.

She fished, gathered seaweed, dried her food on the roof of the boat cabin, and packed it all away until she had a good store.

She made a salve for cuts and soap for her clothes, remembering recipes their housekeeper had used and showed her. She swam every day, sometimes for hours. She found herself eating astonishing amounts of food.

At first she cried a lot. It was hard being completely alone on the water, knowing that she'd have to be alone for some time before she dared come back.

But as she got farther and farther from home, she felt stronger. Maybe *stronger* was the wrong word, because she was already strong. Harder. Like she was developing a shell. She grew big shoulders from rowing and lifting and lowering sails, a powerful body from all the swimming, tough hands from netting and cleaning fish, and a tough mind. And her heart? Completely encased in a locked box. She never cried now, not for anything, not even when she sliced her hand deeply with her knife while gutting a fish. Not even when she thought about her parents and how, in their own ways, neither of them had ever loved her for herself. Not even when she thought about Solomon.

There were no mirrors. Without mirrors, she had no face— only hands and arms and legs, all strong, and she thought they were gorgeous. Sometimes she flexed just to see the muscles move. No one was here to tell her she was ugly, either by words or glance. Even her turned-in feet were so muscled and sundarkened! She loved them. And the fish, glittering under the surface of the water, admired her. Or at least they were curious, for they gathered whenever she swam. They'd not seen humans before—so she was by default the most beautiful and fascinating person they'd ever met. She ate many of them.

She traveled slowly south—the boat moving in spirals and zigzags and meanderings. She didn't really have a goal at first. But as she wandered into the cold southern sea, she discovered something deeply astonishing.

The cold did not bother her.

It was a revelation, like finding out you could fly. It changed everything.

She'd heard stories about cold weather all her life but had never experienced it: biting wind, rain sleeting in icy drops, snow melting when it hit the water but sticking to the roof of the cabin. Raftworld floated in warm weather year-round, following the summer around the globe. Up until now, she'd heard the stories about cold the way one hears fairy tales or ancient history: sure, they might be *true* in some strange way, but probably only metaphorically, and they were never anything you'd actually live through.

But now she floated in the deepening southern winter. And she didn't feel it. At all. Her breath turned to fog, first in the mornings only, and soon all the time. The hairs stood up on her bare arms and legs. It became harder and harder to dry fish properly, and she took to eating raw seafood, cold, which was not as bad as she'd thought it would be. Seaweed froze, and she had to warm it in her mouth to melt it enough to eat.

But she never felt cold.

She considered the phenomenon for days. Weeks. And finally she acknowledged that she had a gift for cold. An actual gift. Magical.

There were people—rare, only a few each generation on all of Raftworld—who had gifts, usually gifts that had something to do with the sea: walking on water, talking to fish, flying with the seabirds—things like that. Amazing gifts that people admired.

She laughed when she finally figured out what was going on. It made sense—in the way that her whole life made sense—that her gift was something no one on Raftworld would value. And that it was a gift that would never even be noticeable until she left Raftworld.

Then she wondered if maybe more people had gifts than anyone realized. What if someone had a gift to—she didn't know—survive on the surface of the sun? Or eat an entire mountain? That person would likely never find out they *had* that gift. What if *everyone* had gifts, but only a rare few ever discovered what their gifts were, because the gifts weren't valued or needed? Rayel spent a couple of days imagining what all the odd gifts might be—things never known because the world didn't ask for them. Maybe there could be someone with a gift to create a universe out of nothing, but only in a place where no humans would live. Or a gift to win a fight, single-handed, against a dragon or some other nonexistent monster. Or . . .

She was grateful she'd found her gift. That she'd gone out and discovered it, in a way. Now she felt more like she was setting off on an adventure and less like she was running away, and it was a good change of feeling.

So she headed south, on purpose now. This amazing cold world belonged to her, thanks to her gift. Why not see how far she could go in it—and find what was out there?

Days passed.

In some ways the landscape didn't change much as she traveled: all around her lay the open sea. But in other ways it did: the sky and water more often took on the look of stone, the kind used on the Island nation of Tathenn for building things, gray and hard. The fish changed—they grew bigger and less brightly colored, and there were fewer of them. The seaweed no longer floated on the surface of the water; she had to net it from deeper; sometimes she dove for it.

The dolphins were slowly disappearing.

She'd seen pods of them all her life, close and far. The friendliest of the fish to humans—even humans who couldn't talk with them, humans like Rayel who didn't have that gift. She loved watching them leap and, when they came close enough, loved hearing them click and call to each other, loved seeing them nose the air and bob their heads at Raftworld. She had often walked to the dock area with Solomon to watch them. He had always waved, and when they leapt, he and she pretended the dolphins were waving back.

But in the colder water there were fewer and fewer dolphins, and when Rayel saw them, they didn't seem to want to stay and play. They were migrating north, just like the birds.

Until one no-breeze day in which the boat lulled, barely moving. She peered down over the edge of her boat, feeling the weak sun on her back and daydreaming into the water. Over the lip of the boat she saw . . . something. Down beneath the surface. Too large to be a fish. Whitish. Not moving.

It was a slow day. Had the wind been blowing, she wouldn't even have noticed the white blob in the water. But as it was, bored, she spotted it and decided immediately to find out what it was.

By this point in the journey, she thought of herself as an explorer. She was going to discover the cold part of the planet and—someday, she'd decided—return triumphant to tell the tale.

Also, she missed human company more than she'd thought she would. She'd even taken to talking to herself.

And this white shape in the water was—something new. Something to connect to. So it was a feeling of loneliness as much as anything else that sent her into the sea.

She stripped and dove for the white shape, unafraid. There hadn't been anything terrible in the water yet; even the stinging jellyfish that she knew from her years on Raftworld had disappeared as the water grew colder. Cold water was friendly water, as far as she was concerned. It was where she belonged.

THE SHAPE turned out to be a baby dolphin, a calf, hovering about ten feet below the surface of the water, caught between life and death. It was pure white—so young it hadn't yet developed its pink underbelly—and almost starved. Horribly, the baby was slashed with five long, deep cuts on its back, parallel marks, as if a monster of some kind had raked long claws across its back.

But there were no such things as monsters.

Rayel wondered where its mother was, and the rest of its pod. And if the wounds on the baby's back had anything to do with this dolphin being—most unusually—all alone. What could have happened?

She swam under it and pushed it up to the surface, where it flipped on its back and gasped shallowly for air. She rubbed its belly and pressed herself against the small body, half her own size, hoping to warm it up. She wasn't sure why she felt so strongly—small things died unfairly all the time; it was how the world worked—but she knew, she *knew* that she couldn't let this dolphin die. That she needed to save this small creature.

Rayel swam away to the boat and returned quickly with her fresh store of fish—caught only an hour ago and meant for her own lunch. The dolphin slurped them down feebly, barely able to summon the energy to swallow. But once it had eaten, it flipped right way up, bumping Rayel with its long nose, its way of saying thank you.

Gently, Rayel rubbed the baby's nose, and the dolphin calf nudged her face and nuzzled under her chin. Rayel's hand slid over the dolphin's head and down its back, stopping as soon as she reached the slashes.

The dolphin stilled so she could inspect the cuts, as if it trusted Rayel to take care of it. Rayel wasn't sure what to do—the wounds looked clean, though deep, and as far as she could tell, there wasn't anything lodged in them. Finally, she swam back to the boat and retrieved the salve she'd made weeks ago, in warmer weather—a simple seaweed gel—and brought a handful of it back to the dolphin, holding it above her head as she treaded water. When she lowered her hand, the dolphin nosed it and then lay on its stomach, the injured area exposed to air, while Rayel applied the poultice. The dolphin floated there for long minutes while she worked, then nudged a thank-you to her again and swam a slow circle around her.

"I think," said Rayel, "we'd better head to warmer waters. At least until you're better." Despite the fact that she wanted to go south, it was not a hard decision to make. She loved the feeling of being needed, and this creature needed her.

BY THE FIRST DAY after they met, Rayel had taken to talking to the dolphin, whom she called, by the second day, Nunu. She didn't *name* the dolphin, exactly; she simply called her by an approximation of the sounds the baby seemed to be making whenever she greeted Rayel. It was possible, Rayel thought, that the dolphin had named *her* Nunu. Or that Nunu meant *hello*.

They traveled, slowly, just far enough north that the steam came from Rayel's breath only in the mornings and disappeared by midmorning. The dolphin grew and healed. She hunted her own food. Her underbelly turned pink and healthy, and the slashes turned into long dark scars in her back.

Rayel had heard stories about dolphins on Raftworld, and in some of the stories dolphins had magic—some of them anyway— and could become human if they wished, if they loved a human enough to transform themselves. And even though she knew these were just fairy tales, Rayel imagined stories about Nunu and told them to her—how Nunu became a princess, or a warrior, or a gardener or schoolteacher or any number of things, transformed by her love for some human. Rayel wove Nunu's scars into the stories sometimes too: Nunu was scarred by a land monster's claws, or by an army invading from the first world with swords, or by a deep sea creature's sharp teeth—sometimes the injury happened when she was in her human form and sometimes in her dolphin form, depending on the story. Nunu seemed to like all the versions. She always nodded.

And as she listened, Nunu healed from her wounds, though slowly. It took weeks for the gashes on her back to close completely. But the dolphin didn't seem to be in pain. She was happy and friendly, swimming up to the boat each morning and bobbing alongside until Rayel let down the anchor and joined her for a swim. Each afternoon Rayel swam with the creature again—they were in no hurry to get anywhere, after all. Rayel learned where the dolphin liked to be scratched and how to hold on to her fin for a ride when she leapt.

The leaping was fantastic.

She found herself pouring out her heart to the dolphin, who seemed to listen. And the dolphin poured her heart out to Rayel—or at least that is what it sounded like. It didn't matter so much that they didn't understand each other. Maybe it even made it easier to talk.

"It's like this," Rayel explained one afternoon as they swam next to each other, Rayel holding Nunu's flipper. "I ran away because I felt I had to—to escape from someone cruel. And there wasn't any reason to stay after Solomon died. I was okay with leaving Raftworld and being all alone—at least, I think I was. But I was lonely. I'm so glad to have found you."

Nunu clicked in agreement.

"Did I ever tell you about the time we ran away from home together? I mean my brother and me."

Nunu clicked again. She was the best listener ever.

"Our mom had . . . scolded us. For something stupid." Nunu didn't ask—she never pressed for more information than Rayel was willing to give—but Rayel sighed anyway and explained. Nunu deserved the whole story. "She was mad because Solomon had graduated from sailing a child-size boat—the kind that's meant only for learning how to use the ropes and how to get up if you capsize—to a regular one-person boat. I mean, she wasn't mad about that. She was mad because . . ."

Why *was* her mother mad, anyway? Rayel massaged the bump on her head, thinking.

"She was mad because he hadn't told her when he got home, and then when the tutor stopped by later to congratulate him, she didn't know anything about it."

But that wasn't really the issue, either. No, their mom was angry because Solomon had told Rayel all about it, and when the tutor stopped by, almost-thirteen-year-old Rayel had said to the tutor, "He's so excited about the big boat. You're a great teacher," just as polite as could be. And the tutor had grinned and clapped Rayel on the shoulder and said, "I should have known you'd draw the story out of him. He adores you."

The tutor had been a nice man—and Rayel hadn't been

wrong to say he was a great teacher. But after that day, Solomon's mom had transferred Solomon into a class with a different sailing tutor, and she'd pulled Rayel aside and told her, tight-lipped, to stop hovering over her brother. Told her she would only bring her brother down. That if she cared about her brother at all, she'd stop embarrassing him by hanging around him all the time.

What exactly, then, had their mom been angry about? She was mad that Solomon had gone to Rayel with his success, that Solomon had thought to tell Rayel before he thought to tell his mother. That his mother hadn't been first—or even on the list at all.

Nunu nudged her. Rayel had been silent too long.

"My mom didn't know that Solomon heard her yelling at me," Rayel said.

Nunu bobbed, her head nodding in the water, and she grinned. She always grinned, so that wasn't a good indicator of listening. But it definitely made her look like she was captivated.

"He found me afterward, crying, and he said we should run away and live by ourselves, just the two of us—and he could sail us there because he could sail a grown-up boat now." She paused to stroke the dolphin's nose. "He was only five. He was adorable."

And so were you, Nunu seemed to say.

"Hah. I was never adorable. But it was . . . cute, I guess, how we thought we could just escape everything. Sail away and live on our own."

Nunu waited, as if asking a question.

Rayel sighed. "It was also stupid, and we knew it as soon as we really tried to leave. We didn't even make it out on the water. We snuck out at night, with some food—not nearly enough—stuffed in our pockets, and we got to the docks and found the boat we were going to steal, and we hid in it until it was really dark, and by then I'd rethought everything. How could I run away with nothing but a pocketful of snacks? And drag Solomon into it? I said we should wait until we were older. That there was more to learn. That if we still wanted to, we could run away together later. And he agreed, because he was cold and tired and wanted to go to bed."

She paused, thinking. Nunu wriggled closer to Rayel's side, and Rayel began to rub her back, fingers bumping over the old deep scars. "That was only one year ago. But it seems so much longer. I thought we were too young to run away then—but now? Now I'm grown and almost married off. And no Solomon." She shrugged away from the thought and wrapped her arm over Nunu's back. "If I'd thought clearly, I probably would have talked myself out of running away this time, too. I'm glad I didn't. And I wish I hadn't talked myself out of it a year ago." *Oh, Solomon.*

If they'd gone last year, he might still be alive.

She shook herself, and Nunu startled. "Sorry."

What were the good things about this trip? She'd met

Nunu. And she'd discovered her gift with cold and could explore the deep south—probably not something she could have done with Solomon, as he likely wouldn't have had her gift.

But . . . going south wouldn't work for Nunu either. Rayel's stomach sank. It was a problem that had been in the back of her mind for a while now. How could she go south and stay with Nunu?

The dolphin flipped back and swam quick circles around her, wanting to play a chase game.

Rayel, in the middle of the circle, treaded water and thought of Solomon. And Nunu. And south.

9

PUTNAM. THE PRESENT.

*I*N THREE more days' time, all Putnam's fresh food was gone—the bread, the fruit, even the carrots. He and Artie netted as much fish and seaweed as they could and dried them on the roof of the boat; this food would keep them going for a long time. What they needed now was more basic. Despite Putnam's care, they were running out of water.

Putnam had lived on the ocean his whole life, and the ocean that he knew contained water—water you could drink. The idea of not being able to swallow what surrounded you—well, that was inconceivable.

But now, first gradually and then suddenly, the water was too bad to drink. Hoping he was wrong, Putnam tasted it once again, but it was so strong with salt and bitterness that he spat it out, retching.

Artie, whittling a stick into a flute, said, "Yeah. I tried it earlier this morning."

He spat again, then took a small swig of their remaining water to clear out the taste.

"We don't have much left," she said.

"Maybe it'll rain."

"We need to find land."

She wasn't wrong. But as far as he could tell, there wasn't any land nearby—which made sense, as the world was mostly ocean. The island of Tathenn—Artie's homeland—was the biggest island in the world, as far as everyone knew. But then, Raftworld never traveled so far south; maybe there were more islands here, maybe even big ones with their own lakes and streams.

And maybe they'd happen across one.

And maybe that was one too many *maybe*s to count on.

Artie brushed wood shavings off her lap. "Meanwhile, we should ration the water we have left." She eyed the two jugs remaining—both of them somewhat brackish from being filled as the ocean's taste worsened. "Or . . . we could head north."

"No," said Putnam. "If I'm going to figure out what's wrong, we need to head south. Besides," he said, trying to get his own way without sounding bossy, which was a fine line to stand on, "if people are looking for either of us, the only direction they won't look is—"

"South," she said. "I thought of that. No one's looking for me. But they might be looking for you by now." She sounded disgruntled.

"Are you wishing I'd stolen a different boat?"

She surprised him by not replying with an outright *yes*. "Partly. But you're . . . not too bad. I mean, the food you brought was good. And you did think to fill the jugs of water."

"Glad to know I'm so wanted." Putnam could feel himself grinning. Artie was trying so hard not to sound like she liked him. But she *did*, at least a little. He could tell. "Well, I'm glad I got on this boat. You're good company."

She ducked her head. Pretended not to hear. But she *did* hear, and a little smile flashed across her face before her hair hid it.

LATER IN THE DAY, the sky cleared to a bright, bright blue, and the sun shone down and glinted from every wave.

They'd been at sea for five days. It had been getting colder as they headed south, but today was suddenly warm again, a last glint of summer before winter. They both lay on the deck, soaking in the rare sunshine. Artie had even shed her outer layers of clothing and was dressed only in leggings and a shirt.

For the first time since the journey had started, Putnam felt sluggish and tired, and the water stretched endlessly in every direction. Before he realized it, the boat had stopped moving.

When he took the oar to steer them back into the current, Artie was staring into the water, at a small bloom of seaweed. "Wait a bit?"

And before he could answer, she dove off the boat and disappeared.

He hadn't wanted to stop. They should be heading south as quickly as possible. Cursing under his breath, he shoved the little craft farther out of the current and dropped the anchor. At that moment, Artie popped up with armfuls of seaweed. Putnam reached to take the plants and climbed on the cabin roof to spread them to dry. They would make good eating later.

When he finished, Artie was treading water, her wet hair pushed back. For once her whole face was visible, almost free now of bruises and filled out with close to a week of good food and sleep.

She looked—happy.

The water was shallow almost everywhere in the ocean, but here it was especially so, the anchor easily reaching the sandy bottom, which Putnam could see in the clear water. There was no coral in sight, but dark beds of seaweed dotted the ocean's floor, and fish darted in and out of the grasses. Putnam saw a small octopus shoot from seaweed to sand, where it quickly changed color to match the floor—and disappeared from sight.

Artie dove and leapt in the water like a dolphin, rising to catch her breath and then shooting back into the water headfirst.

There was something in her face now that reminded him of the first time he'd seen her—at the bonfire. She came up again, gasping, and this time remained at the surface, swirling her arms to tread water. "Come in, the water's fine."

Suddenly Putnam recognized what it was that reminded him of the bonfire. Her face was lit up, glowing. At the bonfire, he'd thought it was a trick of the fire itself—that the fire had given its brightness to her as it did to anyone who came near it. But now he wondered. Maybe she had that glow inside herself, and sometimes it just leaked out—as it did now, in the warm light of afternoon, nowhere near a fire—because she was so focused on something outside herself, so alive to the world around her.

"You could have warned me before you dove off the boat," he said. But that wasn't what he wanted to say, which was: *Why are you suddenly so happy? Why are you diving and smiling?*

"Just a quick break," she said. "Before the water gets so bad we don't want to swim in it."

"Sure," said Putnam. Suddenly he felt happy, too, without being sure why. He tore off his shirt and dove in, resisting the urge to flip in the air on the way down. No need to show off.

ARTIE WAS RIGHT; the water was fine—not nearly as cold as Putnam had thought it would be, given that their nights were quickly becoming frigid.

When they both tired out, they floated near each other on their backs, faces to the last warm fingers of sun. Artie held an empty clamshell half the size of her palm that she'd found on the sand below the water. She seemed to be weighing it in her hand.

"Keepsake?" he asked, turning his head toward her to talk and hear. They were practically lying on top of the water, they were so buoyant. The sea itself was unusually still.

"I was thinking about keeping it for my luck pouch," Artie said, studying the shell.

She wore her luck pouch even in the water—he'd never seen her take it off. "I used to think everyone on the Islands wore the pouches, but it seems like not too many people do," he said.

"Yeah," she said. "It's really only the southerners who dress in the old style anymore. And a few townspeople, I guess, but not many. It's old-fashioned."

"The governor," he said, remembering.

She laughed, but not a nice laugh, and flicked her fingers to make a little splash. "Down south people say, the governor just wants to pretend she's representing all of us. You know what's probably in her luck pouch? Notes for her next meeting. She changes them out every night. And I think she keeps a comb in there, too, for fixing her hair. She's just pretending to live by the old ways." Artie flipped the shell on her chest and filled its tiny bowl with seawater. "But I guess she's okay other than that."

"She said—she's really worried about what's happening with the water."

"She did?"

"Yeah. At the last big session meeting I was at." He could feel a wave of shame wash through his body as he thought of his own dad's reaction. "She wanted to do something about it."

"Is that why you're here? Because you were chosen by that council meeting to go and figure it out?"

Putnam stared up at the sky. There was not a single cloud there, not one. As if everything were clear and pure. Then he turned his head back to talk to her. "Yes," he said. "Yes, they chose me to go." It sounded true. And honorable. And much better than *I ran away because I had a fight with my dad. Because my dad is a coward and bureaucrat.*

"Wow." Artie's voice was suddenly smaller than usual. "That's impressive. They must really trust you." She sounded almost sad.

For a few minutes, they didn't talk. Putnam thought about how the council *didn't* trust him—not even enough to talk openly in front of him. As if he were only a child. And his father certainly didn't trust him. (And now that he'd run away, Putnam certainly wouldn't be trusted again for a long time.)

What Artie was thinking about, he didn't know, but she was silent, too. Eventually, the two floated into each other, bumping shoulders.

Putnam was surprised—he'd almost forgotten for a moment where he was. Artie's face, only inches away, closer than ever before, looked both tough and fragile. The bruises were almost faded away—now simply a greenish and yellowish cast under her skin. The swelling was all gone. Her face was alive with light and thought, the browns of her eyes so dark they were almost black. Close up, she was suddenly beautiful. Herself.

She stared back at him, blinked, and the spell was broken. She kicked her feet and propelled herself away, splashing Putnam at the same time. "*What?*" She sounded almost angry.

"Nothing." He tried to remember what they had been talking about. "Just—well, yes, that's why I'm traveling to the south. To find what made the sea turn salty."

Artie's angry look dropped off her face, and the thoughtful one came back. "There's an Island story," she said, swishing her arms lightly to stay up. Her legs floated out behind her. "About why the water is becoming salt."

I never heard about this. "What is it?" And why hadn't the governor shared it with the council?

"It's a story I heard down south. When I lived there." Her tone did not invite questions about her life, and Putnam didn't ask. "One night this spring, at a bonfire. It was a new story."

"Who told it to you?"

"A fisherman."

Ah. Maybe someone who'd seen something. Island fisher-folk didn't usually take their boats out far from the Island—at least, that was what Putnam had heard—but maybe this person had gone farther and found something out. Putnam was almost disappointed to think so. *He* wanted to be the hero.

"Do you want to hear it or not?" she asked.

"Yes. Of course." Putnam pulled himself back to the present time and place. Everything would work out. She'd tell him something that would help him to understand what had happened. If only he'd thought to ask her sooner.

"Well, I'm not a storyteller, so I can't make it all pretty like they can. I'll just tell you the main points."

"Go ahead." He didn't really need a story, anyway. He just needed an explanation of what had happened, and where to go to fix it.

"So. Long ago the sky and the sea didn't touch. They were separate. There was a space of blue nothingness between them that they couldn't cross. But the sky and the sea liked each other, and they talked across the emptiness every day. The sky would send rain down to keep the sea's fish happy—brand-new water for them to play in and swim in and drink and breathe. The fish would come up to the surface and make little Os with their mouths, blowing kisses to the sky. And the birds—who nap each day on the giant sled that holds up the clouds—"

"The what?"

"It's a winter story, so a sled holds up the clouds."

"But—is the sled the blue sky? What is the sled?"

Artie pursed her lips, then said, "The sled is invisible, okay? It just holds up the clouds. So they don't fall to the ground." Then before Putnam could say more, she said, "It's a *story*. Which you *said* you wanted to hear."

"Right. Sorry."

"So the birds heard the sky wishing to be closer to the sea. And since they *could* cross the nothingness, they swooped down to flutter the sea with their feet, telling the sea how much the sky loved her.

"The sky and the sea were best friends.

"But they wished for more. They wished not to be apart.

"One day the birds and the fish came up with an idea. They built a chain out of seaweed, a long rope connecting the sky and the sea, and they pulled until the two drew together, right through the nothingness, and touched. Held together by a gorgeous, thick green chain that went all the way up to the heavens and down to the bottom of the ocean. And the sky and the sea were happy.

"And then one day—"

"Wait," said Putnam. "Will this story tell me what exactly is wrong and how to fix it? I mean, is it a real story about real things?"

Artie was quiet for a moment. "It's a story about why things went wrong. It might not be *real* real. But it's about real *feelings*."

"Okay. But I mean," Putnam said, struggling to think of how to say it, "is it true information? Or is it just—you know, a story? Like: here's a little-kid fairy tale about the sky and how it loved the fish. Or are you going to say something useful?"

Artie was silent for a long time. Then she said, "Do you want to hear it or not?" She sounded mad, the kind of mad that gets thin tight lips, and even if he said yes, Putnam wasn't sure she'd keep talking.

"I'm sorry. I was rude. I'd love to hear your story."

She narrowed her eyes. "No more interrupting."

"No more." He crossed his hands on his chest in a promise and tried to look completely innocent.

A grin *almost* flashed across her face, Putnam was sure of it. Artie cleared her throat and continued. "Something went wrong. It wasn't the birds, or the fish—it was something else, another creature, maybe even a human—no one knew exactly. But someone broke the chain that attached the sky and the sea, and the chain fell into the sea. And when the chain fell, it yanked part of the sky, and it pulled down the giant sled the clouds ride on—which is made of salt. The sled careened down the sky and landed in the sea, and it's turning the sea to salt as it slowly disintegrates. That's what the fisherman said. To fix it—I guess you'd have to pull the sled out of the sea."

He stared at her. *Seriously?* "You know clouds don't ride on sleds made of salt, right?"

"More like a toboggan."

"They don't."

"I know that," she said in a disgusted voice. "That isn't the point."

What is *the point, then?*

Artie was already climbing back into the boat. "It's just a stupid story," she said over her shoulder.

THEY DIDN'T talk the rest of that afternoon. Putnam was irritated—not angry, he reminded himself, simply irritated—that she'd told such a dumb story. That she'd told it as if it were true. Artie was, he thought, probably irritated—no, *angry*—that he hadn't thought her tale was brilliant.

That night he stayed up late to navigate and star-watch, and then curled up outside the door to the cabin. Inside, a flute played quietly as he huddled to keep out of the wind. He fell asleep to its soft tones. Artie woke early, took one look at him, and told him to go inside to warm up. He slept the rest of the morning in the cabin. The heater made a big difference now that the outside was so cold.

At lunch, when both were properly awake and sitting in the cabin with their coats unbuttoned to the heat, Artie cleared her throat and said, "It's stupid for you to freeze outside at night. You can sleep in here, too. You should."

He felt like he should say no, but it had been so cold last night, his shins were still hurting whenever he touched them. "Are you sure?"

"I just said it, didn't I?"

"Okay. Thanks." Then, because he couldn't resist trying to

lighten the mood: "I appreciate you letting me in the cabin after I stowed away and all."

"As long as you swab the deck every day." She wasn't smiling, but it was a joke. Not a good joke, but then again, he hadn't given her a great deal to work with. They could improve.

"Yes, Captain," he said.

They kept chatting, moving on to small things: Was cooked seaweed tastier than raw? What kind of bird would you want if you could have a pet bird? Things like that. And as they ate, Putnam marveled at how normal everything seemed. She talked to him like he was a friend, not someone she hated for stealing her boat, not someone she feared or admired because he was the king's son. And he was talking to her like she was a friend, not someone who'd been beaten up and burned and starved, not someone who'd run away leaving who-knows-what behind. Just two kids having a normal conversation.

After lunch they went out on deck to check if there was anything to see—any land, any *anything*. There wasn't. Just water all around, colder and colder, more and more salty, less and less friendly-looking.

Artie reached into her luck pouch and pulled out the shell, wrinkling her nose a little. She tossed it lightly in her hand and frowned.

"It's a pretty one," he said. It was. Even dry, the shell glistened, cream-colored with rainbows hiding in it.

She took one more look at it, then threw it in a high arc. It splashed into the water far from the boat and disappeared.

"Why'd you toss it? I mean, if it's okay to ask."

She chose her words slowly. "In your luck pouch, you're supposed to put stuff that is important to you—really important—little objects you might carry around for years and years, and they remind you of the important things that happened to you or important things that you did. *Good* things."

"Like what? What's in yours?"

She shook her head.

Putnam waited.

"That's not a polite question," said Artie. "What's in your luck pouch is private. Unless you choose to tell someone."

"Oh. Sorry." And he was. He'd just ended the longest and pleasantest talk they'd had yet.

"I'm getting cold." Artie went back inside the cabin. The moment was over.

Putnam stayed outside for a while longer. There was truly a bite in the air.

10

ARTIE. THE PRESENT.

*I*T SEEMED like every time she decided maybe he wasn't too bad, he did something nosy and pushy, like he was trying to get to know her. *Know her* know her. Not just "how are you?" kinds of questions but ones that would require her to tell things she didn't want to tell. Say things she didn't want to say out loud.

She just wanted to be left alone. Was it so much to ask?

After he asked what was in her luck pouch, they didn't talk for the rest of the day—not more than *please* and *thank you*. So civil. Putnam slept in the cabin that night, though, and it was good that he did, for even inside, the air was chilled, despite the heater they ran all night long. By morning its battery was nearly dead, only faint heat radiating from the machine.

Artie finished whittling her flute, but she didn't play it. The morning dawned gray and gloomy—the heater battery, attached to the roof of the cabin to recharge, sluggishly sucked up what little sunlight there was. They sat inside, each wrapped in blankets, shivering and hoping the heater would be usable again by night.

After lunch Putnam started chatting about unimportant topics, as if he was trying to bring back yesterday's friendly feel. But Artie had learned her lesson: don't talk about surface stuff, and you won't be asked about deep stuff. She got up without speaking, wrapped the blankets tight around herself like a shroud, and stepped out.

On the deck, she sat against the cabin wall that seemed to be mostly out of the wind and pulled her knees to her chest, tucking the blankets around herself. She stared off into the distance. The ocean was so gray that it melted into the sky, and it was almost impossible to see the faint horizon where the two bodies met. They faded into each other like they were one. Not two separate beings at all.

The answer to Putnam's question was actually very simple. Her luck pouch had nothing in it.

Nothing.

Other people—everyone she knew—had lucky things that had come to them in different ways: a keepsake from a parent, a little reminder of why they had been given the name they had, some small trophy from an important day, tokens of special things and special people.

Her luck pouch had once held something special: a little jeweled ring her mother had worn as a child and had given to Artie just before she died. But this past winter when they were low on food, Artie's stepfather had told her to hand it over. She'd refused. Said she'd rather go hungry. Her stepfather had slapped her and reached right into the pouch as it hung on Artie's neck and taken the ring.

It didn't even buy that much food.

As for any other items in her luck pouch? She'd been waiting, ever since her mother's death, for something to happen, some good sign, that she could keep a reminder of. There were so many bad things or sad things. Some people put things like that in their luck pouches: a lock of hair from someone who'd died, or a snip of a blanket from a long illness. But she wasn't going to. Someday, she told herself, there would be *good* luck. That was what a luck pouch should be for. Remembering the good past. Not the bad.

But there never was any good luck. There was only her, standing up for herself and getting beaten down. And standing up again.

And then she ran away, and she felt like maybe her luck might change, and when she found the shell and saw its gleam inside, like a cleaned bone but shimmering, she felt like maybe her luck had changed—and the shell might be a sign of it. But in the light of the next day, she thought, *No.* Things could still go wrong. She wouldn't collect anything until she was *sure.* Then there would be an item so right, so obvious, that it would of course go in her luck pouch.

Until then, it would hang empty around her neck, a little container of nothing. Just like herself.

SHE SAT FOR A LONG TIME, knees pulled to her chin, blanket wrapped around her to make a cocoon, head poking out, facing seaward.

Then she startled.

What was that?

The invisible place where the gray sea met the gray sky . . . now had a dark line on its border. But only in one spot: a dash— sitting right where the horizon should be.

She squinted, then stood and shadowed her eyes with her hand, even though the sun wasn't out. It didn't help. The short line on the horizon neither disappeared nor grew fatter. It remained a black dash, fuzzy in the distance.

Artie swung into motion. The way they were moving with the current, they would miss it—and *it* was the first possible is- land they'd seen since they left her homeland. She grabbed the rudder and steered them out of the current. The current was wider now than it had been—no longer the narrow stream that Putnam had stumbled on so many days ago—and it took her several long minutes to get into still water.

She began to hoist the sails, setting them to catch the wind and zigzag the boat toward the thing on the horizon.

Putnam popped open the cabin door and came out, rubbing his eyes like he'd just woken from a nap. "What's going on?"

She forgot to frown. "I think we found land."

11

RAYEL. ABOUT 100 YEARS EARLIER.

*R*AYEL AND Nunu stalled for a few weeks in the brisk water of the not-quite-south while Nunu's health improved. Meanwhile the weather grew colder even though they weren't moving south. Rayel guessed this meant winter was coming—something she'd never lived through before. The dolphin, healthy and fat and closer to full size after weeks of rest, began to grow agitated. When Rayel left the boat to swim with her—which she did for hours every day—Nunu tried to get her to swim north, and when she climbed back into the boat, the dolphin clicked in a distressed manner and circled the boat uneasily.

One morning Nunu wasn't there when Rayel awoke. The girl stood on the deck and called for the dolphin, and the dolphin didn't come. She didn't know what to do. What could have happened? Could Nunu simply have left her? She waited all morning, more and more worried—and a little angry. After all she'd done. After she'd put off going south.

Around noon, the dolphin returned, swimming in from the west, leaping in the sunshine. She swam up to the boat and didn't even listen to Rayel's relieved scolding, interrupting her to call and click and bob her head in the direction she'd come from.

Rayel was confused. What could be out there? But the dolphin clearly wanted her to follow.

And it wasn't as if following the dolphin would take her farther away from her goal: they'd be heading west, not north. It would be just a detour, before Rayel had to make the decision she felt tugging at her stronger and stronger: to go south. With her gift for cold, she knew south was where she belonged.

She pulled anchor and trimmed the sails and headed west, following the dolphin, who shot ahead and then came back, urging her forward over and over throughout the day. Finally Rayel saw, ahead on the horizon, what the dolphin had been pointing her toward.

An island.

It was big—far bigger than one person needed. When she entered the bay, she realized what might be attracting the dolphin: the water in the bay was warmer, by quite a bit, than the rest of the ocean. Maybe there was a warm spring feeding into it from the island. Warm water didn't matter to Rayel, but to the dolphin it would feel heavenly. Here was somewhere they could both spend the winter—before Rayel headed south again.

And maybe in the spring, the weather would turn warm enough for Nunu to head south with her.

Maybe.

Rayel didn't want to think about what might happen— that at some point she might get so far south and cold that Nunu wouldn't be able to come with her even in summer, that at some point Rayel might have to choose between south and her friend.

THEY SPENT THE NIGHT in the water of the bay, the dolphin warm but uneasy. Rayel wasn't sure why, but she felt uneasy, too. The shore around the bay looked forbidding, with trees crowding the beach and leaning toward her like accusers. The narrow beach was empty and the bay silent except for the light splashing of waves on the sand. The next day, Nunu swam around the island, checking it out, while Rayel dove and swam in the bay. However eerie the island might be, the seaweed here was thick and healthy, and there were lots of fish. She might not even need to go ashore for food.

She found herself glancing often at the shore. Once in a while, she'd hear a birdcall, but never a call she recognized. Other than that, silence. Like the island was waiting. She had the creepy sensation that something—or someone—was watching her. But each time she looked, no one was there.

Late in the afternoon, Nunu returned, and the whole dream of staying at the island for the winter was over. Nunu was terrified. She nudged the boat, then rammed it, clicking and whistling, until Rayel finally pulled up anchor and left the bay. They headed east again, and when the island was out of sight, Rayel put down anchor and sat, deep in thought, on the deck, while the dolphin clicked and called from the water.

She didn't know why they'd left the island, but she knew Nunu was trying to tell her there was danger, and she trusted the dolphin. Something about that place not only wouldn't work, but terrified Nunu—something made her pink underbelly turn pale with fright, made her clicks so high-pitched they hurt Rayel's ears. The long scars on her back had never looked so dark and clawlike. Rayel wondered if the thing that had hurt Nunu was on that island. Was that it?

Whatever it was, it was something Nunu couldn't say, at least not so that Rayel could understand it. But it didn't matter. Rayel felt it, too. There was something dangerous on that island.

The dolphin shimmered in the water; it looked like she was shivering. A layer of slush floated on the sea's surface.

It was time to decide which direction to go.

12

*W*HEN PUTNAM understood why Artie was turning the boat, he didn't try to stop her, but he also didn't join in to help. He should have been happy to see the island—overjoyed, even, since they were so short on water and it was the first land they'd seen. But he wasn't happy.

Part of his problem was that the island wasn't south; it was west. And the adventure he wanted was south; this was a detour and would cost time. But an even bigger reason was that something—he could not explain what, even to himself—felt wrong about this island. And it felt more wrong the closer they got.

Artie was excited. "We can get out of the cold for a bit. And maybe find some food that isn't fish. And there will be water!" They were down to their last container, and although they'd gotten good at collecting rainwater, it hadn't rained in several days. They were running out.

So why did he feel so odd—so *wrong*—about turning and stopping at the island? Artie trimmed the sails and zigzagged them toward shore.

It wasn't because of the island. The island was . . . an adventure. Somewhere no one from Raftworld had ever been, Putnam was sure.

No, he guessed it was simply the fact that they were turning from their path. The fish had told his dad to find the source of the salt in the deep south. Knowing that, of course Putnam wanted to go there. But he felt also like something was pulling him southward, and not just because he wanted to solve the mystery of the salt water. He *did* want to solve it, but that wasn't what was pulling him. He felt sick to his stomach to turn away, even briefly, from their southward movement.

And turning toward the island . . . worried him.

There was no way to explain this feeling to Artie without sounding crazy. So he kept it to himself.

Eventually artie became impatient. "Could you maybe help?" She was struggling with a sail that had come loose.

Putnam came over to steer, but sluggishly. And after a few moments, Artie took the rudder back. "I thought people on Raftworld knew how to guide small boats. But I guess I was wrong."

Putnam couldn't even bring himself to argue. His stomach

hurt more and more as they turned away from the south and headed west toward the . . . well, it was definitely an island.

As they drew nearer, the land popped out of the horizon and became a hilly outcropping covered with what Putnam thought of as "cold weather trees," oak and maple and birch and all kinds of firs. Trees like you might find on Artie's big island—though this island looked smaller than hers.

Still, it was plenty big enough for the two of them.

It stood fairly low to the water. The main Island of Tathenn, where Artie had lived, jutted out of the water with rock cliffs, except that the capital city had a large bay, and the southern part of the island had some long sandy beaches. These were the good places to launch a boat for fishing or traveling. Other parts of the island were not easily accessible by water—unless you liked to climb steep cliffs. *This* island, on the other hand, looked to be all beach, at least on the eastern side. They could land wherever they wanted.

But as they got closer (Artie muttering all the time about Putnam being lazy), Putnam could see that maybe he was wrong, and most of the island was encircled by rocky cliffs. They were approaching a large bay that made up the entire eastern side of the island: from this side, the island was crescent-shaped, and they were sailing toward the curved inside of the crescent. The north and south of the island, on the other hand, appeared to rear up to the sky and probably weren't easy to land on. Putnam and Artie had gotten lucky. They'd be able to drop anchor in the calm bay waters.

It was dusk by the time they reached the bay, where they lost the breeze and stalled. Artie wanted to row in and beach the boat before night. Her face was alight with excitement, as if this island were the very thing she was looking for. But she hadn't known it would be here. She had just been running away—she hadn't made a plan. Not like him.

Putnam felt a surge of resentment for Artie and for her excitement. They should be sailing south.

On top of all that, it was a bad idea to land on a strange island at night. "We need to wait until morning." He tried to make his voice sound calm.

She snorted. "We should land now. We'll be able to explore a little, even, before nightfall. And have a bonfire. Think how good that will feel."

It was cold, even in the bay away from the ocean's direct wind. There were white patches on the shore that Putnam was pretty sure were snow—not that he'd ever seen snow before, but he'd heard stories from Tathenlanders.

Which meant Artie would know. "Snow?"

She squinted. "Yeah. Probably." Then she shrugged. "It'll be warmer under the trees."

"No," he said. "Listen, I agreed to come here even though

it's a detour for me, because you wanted to see the island. But we're not landing at night. We don't even know what's out there." *Or who,* he almost added.

"What, like monsters?" she said. "Seriously?" But he glared at her like he'd seen the Island governor do—like he wished his dad would do sometimes—and he did not back down.

She darted a glance toward shore. "Fine. Tomorrow morning, as soon as it's light."

EVENING ON the boat was quiet. They both felt edgy, and neither of them knew how to put it into words. Seeing the island brought back memories for them both, and not good ones. Putnam thought of his mom leaving long ago, and of the recent fight with his dad. Artie remembered her mom's death, and she remembered her stepfather throwing a pan of oil at her, and she remembered his fists, and she remembered his open hands. Somehow staring at the island in the dusk made all these memories sharper for both of them. Worse.

Putnam said, "It reminds me of something . . . another island, maybe . . ."

Artie, who'd never been to any island but her own, nodded. "Yeah."

"The smell . . ." said Putnam.

"And the sound," said Artie.

"It's like—it's like *something*." He shrugged. "I'm sure

it's just because it's dark. You know. Creepy. It'll all be fine tomorrow."

Artie went into the cabin, and after a moment, Putnam followed.

THEY RESTED in the boat in the big silent bay that night. On the floor across the cabin from him, Artie snored. Putnam couldn't doze off.

The island curved around them, and it didn't feel comforting to him. It felt ominous. But then, he told himself, he'd lived all his life on a giant raft, so it made sense that land wouldn't call to him the way it did to Artie. Still, this land felt . . . wrong, somehow.

Or maybe it was just that they weren't moving south anymore. He could feel a pain growing stronger in his gut, the longer they stayed away from their southern path: a cramped-up feeling that made him want to curl on the floor and whine. An invisible key wound up his insides like a clockwork, so that his hands kept twitching all by themselves, and his heart raced and his lungs felt tight. He should be going south. There was something there, calling to him.

*No, not something. It feels like some*one.

THE NEXT morning, Putnam woke from a light, disturbed sleep. His stomach still hurt, but the pain felt dulled. Fog hung in the air like curtains. They could see only a short distance in any direction. They steered gingerly toward shore, Putnam carefully rowing in the back while Artie stood on the prow and watched for rocks or sandbars.

There were too many rocks and fallen logs to land the boat.

When they were a short distance out from shore, they decided together that they were as close as they could safely get, and frigid as the water was, they'd swim the rest of the way. Putnam stripped down to his shorts, placing his clothes in a waterproof sack that he strapped to his back. Into the sack he also placed three more waterproof bags—to hold any fresh water they might find—along with a handful of bright yarn strings snipped from the edge of a blanket, a piece of flint, and a small knife.

Artie packed nothing. She removed her top layer and handed it to him to put in the bag, but kept her leggings and shift on: "I'll dry."

And they dove. The water was so cold there were little chunks of slush in it, and for a moment, Putnam thought he'd seize up and not be able to swim. But then, wonderfully and painfully, his muscles quivered to life, and he pummeled himself toward shore, reaching it in time to shake the water off and drag his clothes onto his damp body. Artie followed and huddled on the sand, shivering.

The sun was beginning to break up the fog, but even so the air was chilled. Putnam said, "I'll build a fire." His teeth clacked.

Artie shook her head. "We'll warm up as we explore." Her lips were tinged with blue.

"It'll take ten minutes."

Artie didn't move as he piled up driftwood and pulled his flint out of the waterproof sack. He wasn't sure she *could* move. When he'd gotten the blaze started, she held her hands toward it and, after a few minutes, stood and rotated as if she were trying to cook herself evenly. Her clothing steamed.

A short time later, when the first big logs of driftwood were ashing down to ghosts, Artie said, "I feel much better." She grinned. "I'm going to explore now."

"Let me put out the fire, and I'll join you."

"No!" she said, and then maybe realizing she sounded too stern, she added, "It'll be quicker if we go in different directions."

"We need water," Putnam said. "Fresh water. And fruits or vegetables if we can find any. But we don't want to stay on the island. This isn't where the water's gone bad—we need to keep going south as soon as possible." He was trying not to sound desperate. He tried to sound like he knew what he was doing. Like he was in charge.

She said, "Water," nodding, but didn't add anything else.

"If we split up, we need to meet back here before nightfall."

"We could stay a few days."

"No." Now Putnam thought he might sound too strong, too bossy. "I mean, we need to leave, to get south. And there's something about this island. . . . I think we're better off sleeping on the boat."

She shrugged, clearly more comfortable with land than he was.

"Meet back here before night. At least an hour or so before sundown."

"Sure."

Artie picked up one of the waterproof sacks they'd packed with them and stalked off. She climbed to the top of a small dune, then turned back. "I'm heading this way," she said.

"I guessed that," said Putnam.

"So you go a different way." She turned and disappeared down the far side of the dune, aiming for the woods.

"Like I couldn't figure that out," muttered Putnam.

He was talking to himself; Artie was long gone. He shook his head quickly to clear it, hoping to make himself feel more optimistic. It didn't work. This place just felt wrong, and Artie going off on her own felt wrong, too.

What else could he do besides explore, though? He had all day, and they needed some fresh water. He took the other three waterproof sacks and headed the other direction. Away from the beach. Away from their little boat, anchored offshore. Away from where he knew he should be going: south.

WHEN PUTNAM entered the woods, he felt what he always, at some point, felt on solid ground: that the land was both too quiet and that small noises were too loud. Without the constant background of waves and the wind, each birdcall surprised him, each footfall echoed. And everything was a little claustrophobic, the open sea too far away. The forest was old growth—it had never been cut for wood, at least as far as he could tell—and mostly pine. Dead trees lay on the ground, and live ones stretched their spindly arms to the sky. Light filtered through in shards. Needles crunched underfoot, and the spaces between the trees seemed empty and waiting.

There were no paths, not even the crisscrossing tracks of small animals. Maybe the needled woods couldn't hold paths.

And definitely there wouldn't be any human trails. There were only two countries in the whole world, and neither the Islanders nor the Raftworlders had ever been to this cold little southern island before—Putnam was sure of that.

He found a good stream early on and drank until he almost felt sick. Then he filled the water sacks. They were too heavy to carry all day, so he left them against a tree with a bright yarn tied around to tag it so that he could find the sacks on the way back to the boat.

Remembering how the Raftworld storyteller once told about how to find your way in the woods, he marked his trail as he went, scuffing his feet in the needles and breaking small branches to show the way. He tied a small piece of yarn every few minutes, and looked back often to see if he could spot the marker behind him. The Islanders had an old, old story about a boy and a girl—siblings, in the story—who'd gone into the woods and gotten lost, and they'd found a terrible monstrous witch who tried to eat them. He knew that wouldn't happen here—for one thing, there was no such thing as witches. *No such thing.* But as he created his trail, his mind kept falling back to that tale and the bread-crumb path that didn't help those children. The birds ate the crumbs. He couldn't remember how the story ended—which bothered him.

He hoped to find a high spot where he could survey the island. Finally he climbed a long, gradual hill at the top of which the trees thinned to nothing, just a windy meadow of long grasses, now brown and matted in the coming winter. There were patches of snow in the shade of a few big rocks. The field looked almost sullen. He shivered despite the effort of the climb.

Putnam found a dry sunny spot and lay on the ground to get out of the wind. His face to the sunshine, he felt immediately better: he could see nothing but sky, and he could almost pretend he was at sea again. Even the wind, much stronger on the hilltop meadow, was comforting; its sound reminded him of the water. A lone spider crawled up a tall grass next to him, and he thought of all the spider tales he'd heard as a small kid and was comforted. Spiders were clever, and they usually did okay in the stories. He closed his eyes.

And felt . . . something.

No: *heard* something. A sound so deep and so quiet it almost felt like a tremble of the earth. He pressed his hands to the ground and opened his eyes. The earth couldn't be trembling. The *sea* moved. Land didn't.

The field wasn't moving. But there was a rumbling, low and quiet, somewhere. Slowly he lifted his head and looked around. Then he flipped over, crouching in the brown grass and scanning the meadow and the trees around the meadow's edge. Nothing. And the sound was gone now, too.

He lay back down, and there it was again, a low rumble, as if the earth's stomach were growling. And there was something, a shifting feeling, to this ground. He was sure of it.

This time he hopped up quickly, looked around again, and decided it was time to go. Heading back down to the bay, he forced himself not to run, to be careful and find each yarn string as he retraced his trail back to the boat. But what he wanted to do was scuttle as quickly as possible to reach the safety of the water. He felt like there was something watching him. Some*one* watching him. Following him.

He reached the shore much earlier than he and Artie had

agreed, and spent the afternoon there, near the water, building a small raft they could pole back to the boat, which still floated hopefully in the bay. Putnam was expert at building rafts; all the kids on Raftworld had constructed them as babies, practically, assembling little floats, capsizing them and building them again. This one he made of driftwood and fallen branches, lashed with vines and caked with mud to become as strong as possible, even though it only needed to last for a single short trip. It would last much longer than that, as solidly as he built it.

And the work kept him busy.

By late afternoon, one hour before sunset, he was sitting on the raft on the water's edge, scanning the woods for Artie. She was nowhere to be seen.

13

ARTIE. THE PRESENT.

*A*S SOON as she dried off enough to stop shivering, Artie threw on her top layer of clothes and left both the fire and Putnam behind to explore the island. She was glad to leave. Bonfires on the beach, as warm and comforting and let's-have-a-party-with-our-friends as they were supposed to be, also reminded her of her old life: the village bonfires where, after her mother's death, Artie's stepfather hung out night after night arguing politics and getting angrier and angrier—even while laughing and joking. His tone seemed jovial and good-humored, but the words were complaining and sometimes mean. Bonfires, to Artie, meant her stepfather telling "funny" stories about how the Island's southerners were ignored, how fisherfolk were overlooked, and how now he had to raise some girl who wasn't even his. And she sitting off to one side feeling the words jab or sneaking away alone, hoping he'd forget to come home that night.

Bonfires weren't comforting.

Leaving Putnam, on the other hand, made her feel a little bad. Sure, he was a rich kid with a perfect life and no real problems to his name, and his mission (if you could even call it that) was kind of ridiculous. Who trusted that kind of trip to a kid, even the son of a king? He wasn't a bad person, though. He was actually pretty nice, most of the time, and he had been okay to travel with. His company wasn't terrible.

But her plan had been to escape to a place where she could be alone. Alone was best if you wanted to be safe: no one to disbelieve you, no one to make you go back home.

She wasn't going to return to the boat. She was going to stay, alone, on the island. She'd spend the day exploring and scouting for a temporary new home—a dry cave if possible. She'd collect wood and figure out how to live through the winter. She'd need to start drying fish and seaweed immediately. So for the next few weeks, storing up food would be her first priority; when the water froze over—as it looked like it might—she needed to have enough food to make it through the winter.

Fortunately she was scrawny and didn't need much. And she was used to being hungry.

ARTIE DISCOVERED a stream that emptied into a small pond and tasted the water: clean and cold and pure. Good.

Water was taken care of. She hung the empty water sack on a tree above that pond so that she could retrieve it after she'd found a place to live.

She picked up a walking stick; it was the perfect length and weight and feel. She found some late berries—snowberries, just like on Tathenn—and ate her fill of them, mentally marking their location so that she could come back later and gather more and dry them. She found something that almost resembled a trail—though that wasn't possible, since no one lived on this island—and followed it uphill until she came upon a rocky cliff that stood against the sea. A path seemed to wind down the cliff toward the water.

Hmm. Maybe she *had* been following a small animal route; she'd seen rabbits and ground squirrels, and they could make trails. Maybe there were caves in this cliff—little ones for rabbits or snakes, and maybe even a bigger one just the right size for herself.

She followed the smooth dirt almost-a-path that wound through the big rocks and over the side of the cliff, where there was a definitely-a-path that zigzagged downhill—maybe made by water trickling down the rock face over the years.

Partway down the cliff, she found it. A cave. A cave just the right size for someone like her.

She sat outside for some time, soaking up the sun and leaning against the cliff wall. But she wasn't just resting. No, she was doing exactly what you should do when you find a cave big enough to fit—well, anything alive. She was waiting.

When she'd been there for the better part of an hour, listening, she picked up a few rocks and tossed them into the opening, where she heard them hit walls and crack to the ground. Nothing.

Then she stood at the mouth of the cave and peered in. She couldn't see far, as the cave hooked around. But it appeared empty, though astonishingly clean. There must have been something living here at some point, keeping the entryway free of brush and dirt. She tossed a few more rocks in, aiming in different directions and listening for any sounds in response.

There was nothing but silence, and the day was getting later. The afternoon sun slanted across the entry, very little of it spilling inward.

She took a deep breath. This was what she wanted. A quiet empty place all to herself. A place where she would be safe.

She entered the cave.

THE BOAT, she knew, had a small torch that gathered sunlight during the day and used it up at night, but she didn't have any such thing with her, so after she entered the cave (she didn't even have to stoop, the doorway was so tall), she sat in the shadows for a while, facing away from the doorway and letting her eyes adjust to the murky darkness.

As the cave slowly appeared before her eyes, she liked what she saw. Straight dry walls and a smooth floor and ceiling. This cave was old but sturdy—not in danger of collapsing. And the entryway was high enough that a bonfire laid there would provide some heat without sucking out all the oxygen. But maybe she wouldn't even need much fire to make it through the winter, if the cave went far enough in and stayed warm enough on its own. Already, only a few feet in, it felt warmer than outside.

She put her hand on one of the smooth walls and walked slowly into the darkness, sliding her feet carefully along the ground. Around the curve the cave was dark, but not completely black, as there was a small opening high up that let in some light—and some air, which was good. Air could go bad in a cave, and vents were a good thing.

A little farther on, she could hear the musical tinkle of water, and she kept following the curve (and the slight downward bent of the tunnel) to find a small dribble—a tiny spring—that popped out of the wall from a spout, pooled in a basin about two feet across, and drained slowly back into the cliff. The whole area of the cave widened here, as if to make a kitchen for her, a low flat rock in the corner standing like a table. A thin shaft of light fell on the table from a vent above. The water in the tiny spring gurgled. Scooping her hands under the spout, she tasted the water. Sweet. She lowered her head and drank deeply. Perfect.

Then she moved on, following the curve of the cave into shadows—a gradual downward spiral, it seemed—thinking what all this meant. This cave could not be better suited for a human to live in. For *her* to live in. She felt as if it had been waiting for her.

As she followed the downward coil of the tunnel, the light waned to almost complete darkness, but she could see something before her—around the curve, another little bit of light ahead. She crossed her fingers and made a wish—which she *never* did, never. But something about this place seemed almost magical. So she wished: what she needed now was a cozy bedroom where she could pile some straw and spend the winter in comfort. With a bedroom, the place would be perfect.

When she turned the corner, another high skylight overhead showed her that what she had wished for did, indeed, exist.

It was a bedroom, small and cozy and already completely lined with a thick layer of straw, the dried grasses piled up high and warm. Like magic.

And in the middle of the straw: two hollows, as if two bodies had napped there. Large bodies. So large, in fact, that sleeping bodies *couldn't* be what the dents came from. People didn't take up that much room, not even if they were enormous grown-ups.

Artie stood perfectly still at the juncture where the tunnel ended and the little room opened up like a fist at the end of an arm. Why the dents in the straw? Why the straw at all? Up until now she could tell herself that the cave just happened to be here, in this condition, that she was just—finally, finally—lucky. The clean cave, the openings at exactly the right places, the warmth even without a fire, the big stone like a table. But a bed? And a bed that looked like it had been slept in? She felt her heart beating in her throat. She felt suddenly like she could hear the walls breathing. Slowly she backed up.

And then she heard something—a shuffling, like feet padding gently along a cave floor. And breathing—loud breathing, almost panting, as if something much bigger than she was (or maybe there were simply *more* of them) was moving toward her.

The noise didn't come from behind her. It came from somewhere in front of her—from the bedroom. No, from *behind* the bedroom. She peered into the shadows and then saw it across from her: a crack, an extra corner, barely visible in the half-light. The bedroom had another entrance, and someone was coming toward that entrance.

She stood, frozen, for a couple seconds longer. She told her feet to move, but they did not move. What was coming toward her felt like everything she'd run away from, and now it was about to get her. It had followed her across the ocean. She almost imagined she *knew* who was coming toward her, but she couldn't know; he couldn't have followed her; this was a new danger, but it felt exactly like old danger, like danger she knew, and she couldn't make her feet move, and she couldn't get away.

"GO." It was a whisper, but a loud one. It came from her own mouth.

Immediately the panting stopped, like the Thing was listening. Had heard her. And then the feet padding started up again, this time louder and faster, and the panting filled her ears. She turned and ran, as fast as she could, up the cave and out into the cold air, scrambling over the rocks to the top of the cliff. The world flying by so fast. So fast. So fast. She wasn't even breathing, not thinking anymore, just running and running from whatever it was in the cave.

At the top of the cliff she almost fell—a quick stumble before she caught herself on a rock, cut her hand open, and gasped with the pain. As she righted herself, she glanced back over her shoulder, just one hasty look, and what she saw was almost enough to make her turn to stone right there.

Following her: two enormous bears, snowy white, with claws the size of her face. They were staring up at her from the mouth of the cave. As she looked, one lifted its head and roared. She felt hypnotized. The bear lowered its nose and stared at her, snuffling, and she could see the hatred in its dark eyes as it slowly shook its shaggy head. Then it roared again, rearing back on its hind legs and raking the air, and when it landed, it started lumbering up the cliff. Not quickly. Leisurely. As if it were playing a game—a game it knew it could win. The other bear followed.

The bears' movement toward her broke the spell. Artie unfroze and ran. She did not look back again—she just ran, straight through the forest back to the beach, hoping against hope that Putnam had waited for her, expecting at any moment to feel five sharp slices across her back.

AS THE woods thinned near the bay, Artie still raced as fast as she could, but she wheezed heavily now and almost stumbled with every step. Her chest burned and her side pinched. She looked back over her shoulder again: she couldn't see the bears, but she could hear them, panting heavily in rhythm with her own gasping. She could hear them inside her own head, growling. And she could feel, in the old burns on her arms and chest, their claws digging deep. They were near.

Putnam stood knee-deep in the water with a raft half pushed out to sea, as if he'd been about to leave. Artie was very late. The sun was setting, its red light splashed across the sky as its round head tipped below the horizon.

Putnam stared at her, a *what's wrong?* in his face, as she flew across the beach, gasping. She didn't answer. Couldn't talk. She leapt on the raft and collapsed, motioning wildly for him to set off. Wordlessly, he did, his motions quick and his face worried.

When he'd poled them a good halfway to the boat, he said, "What is it?"

Artie shook her head. She still couldn't talk, and now she felt sick. She leaned over the raft and threw up, heaving until there was nothing left in her stomach. Finally she stood to take the other pole.

"Rest," said Putnam. "I can do it."

She shook her head. "Faster." Still panting, and now wobbly and sick, she helped direct them to the boat. The shore, meanwhile, looked empty, but she knew they were there. Somewhere. Watching.

When they reached the boat, she scrambled aboard and stood clutching her pole until Putnam, who'd climbed aboard with his three bulging water containers, pried the pole from her fingers and dropped it in the bay, placing her hand on the boat's railing. "We don't need the raft now. We'll leave it behind."

She nodded, staring at the shore.

Putnam raised the anchor and set up the sails. Artie felt a little like she should help, but she couldn't move. She still felt sick. She clutched the rail, and when her legs gave way, she sat, staring through the bars at the vacant shore of the island.

When the boat was slowly moving out of the bay, he

returned to stand next to her. "What happened?" He coughed. "I thought—I was worried you weren't coming back."

Suddenly he froze. The monsters were on the beach: two white bears, even larger than she remembered them, lumbering from the woods and hulking on the shore. One nudged the other and gestured its head toward the water, and they waded out into the bay. They stood chest-deep in the water, and Artie knew they were looking at her. She just knew.

Putnam, next to her, gulped audibly. When he spoke next, after a long silence, his voice sounded pinched. "Oh. Oh, I see. Wow." He put his hand on top of hers, and it was so warm and alive and human that she didn't jerk her own hand away. "That's what was . . . chasing you?"

She nodded.

"What happened?"

"They just . . ." She didn't want to say everything, but she could tell at least part of it. "I *was* going to stay. I liked that island, and I thought it would make a good home. They chased me." She couldn't bring herself to tell how scared she was, how she'd heard them the whole way—how she still heard them, growling inside her somewhere.

"You're safe now," said Putnam, and sat with his shoulder pressed against hers.

I'm not. I'm never safe. They watched the bears, one now

pacing back and forth on shore, the other still chest-deep in the bay, both of them shrinking smaller and smaller as the boat drifted away. The abandoned raft floated between the bears and them like a tiny patch on the ocean's sleeve.

14

RAYEL TRIED to explain to Nunu why they needed to go south, but more than ever she felt the limits of language. Nunu clicked and whistled, and Rayel explained, for days on end, the water and air around them slowly growing colder. She told Nunu, again, about her gift for the cold and how she had to follow it to the end, to see how much she could withstand and how far she could explore. She owed it to the gift. But her words upset Nunu.

The dolphin was desperate to go to warmer waters. She grew thinner in the cold water, her whistles sounding almost like sneezes. Rayel couldn't bring herself to go north—but couldn't leave her friend, either. They were stuck. The weight rested on Rayel's chest, pressing down on her heart. No matter what she decided, it would be the wrong decision.

Then one morning, Nunu was gone.

She'd made the choice that Rayel couldn't and had left in the night. Rayel waited all day to see if she'd return. But she didn't.

Two mornings after that, Rayel headed south.

Alone. Again.

RAYEL WAS UPSET. Of course she was. She missed Nunu terribly. But she was also grateful; by leaving, the dolphin had given her permission to head south.

Rayel had never been special before, not at anything, not ever. She was the opposite of special, except to her brother, and maybe to Nunu, who had never seen a human before and therefore thought she was magical.

But here it was: with this gift for cold, she suddenly *was* special . . . but only if she stayed in cold parts of the world. She could survive where no one else could. She wore the same summer shift she'd started her voyage in, and she used the blankets to provide more cushion to her bed but not to cover herself up. She was warm all the time. Or maybe, more to the point, she wasn't cold. Ever.

WEEKS LATER, when Rayel saw her first icebergs, she didn't know what they were. All of a sudden, the horizon broke up into jagged humps: elbows and sharp corners. And as she sailed among them and dove and swam around them, she learned that some were just slabs of floating ice, and others—more worrisome for a boat—were giant craggy chunks that descended like mountains well below the surface, showing only their icy peaks above water. She pulled in her sails and began to row, winding between them. Soon she found a current that took her slowly southward, leaving her free to steer, with her paddle like a rudder. Icebergs rose like towers above her. She looked around in awe.

Yet she wasn't cold. Not a single shiver. The ice towers creaked. The birds had long since disappeared, and she couldn't see any fish in the water, but she felt . . . fine.

Rayel couldn't feel the cold; but maybe it was more correct to say that the cold couldn't feel her. That was what it seemed like, anyway: the cold was out there, searching for something warm and alive to torment, and it walked right past her, not even realizing that she was there. It didn't find her and freeze her, and she slipped through it safely.

She missed Nunu all the time. If she hadn't been so toughened by now, she would have cried.

OVER THE NEXT FEW WEEKS, alone on the craft and steering into worse and worse weather, she wondered how smart her logic was. What if, for example, she had never discovered her gift? Would she still have a duty to follow it? And what if (to return to her earlier daydream) her gift had been something crazy: to survive on the surface of the sun? Would she have the duty to follow *that* adventure to its end? Did a gift naturally bring with it the duty to use the gift? Or could a person, say, turn the gift down and go north with the dolphins?

But Nunu was long gone, so there was no reason to go back. And there was something exciting about being the first explorer to ever find the true south. Rayel kept going.

When she finally reached land, she wasn't even sure at first that it *was* land. There was by now so much ice everywhere that she was constantly navigating through it. She moved mostly by latching onto slow currents and steering between icebergs. The water was deeper than she'd ever known water could be, so deep that she couldn't see to the bottom, where it grew black. Food was scarce; she was eating her dried stores, which was a worry.

She'd see what there was here to see, then turn back north and find food. She anchored, roughly, to a giant shard of ice and dove into the water, swimming the short distance to shore, where she shook off as much water as she could before it froze into her clothes. Glad for her light boots because of the sharp ice, she climbed a long, low hill and stared in every direction. The land was empty of anything but snow and ice. It was beautiful— and more colorful than she would have imagined. Under the bright blue sky, the land rolled out in dunes. The snow, crusted by time and wind into small regular waves, glinted blue with purple shadows. Far off, a patch of clear ice glowed green.

Distance was impossible to judge.

And—what was *that*? Near the horizon was . . . something.

A mound of snow containing a lighted circle, like the opening to a cave, except bright. It glimmered for just a moment as the sun hit it, then disappeared into the dimming and purpling snow. She wanted to know what it was, but the day was quickly waning. A goal for tomorrow. She shivered with excitement (not cold) and headed back to the boat.

The next morning, however, she woke to loud cracking. The boat, as if it had simply given up upon reaching shore, creaked and boomed and finally broke apart around her, crushed by the ice. While it was still groaning, she scrambled and brought out her food stores and everything she thought might be necessary. Then she stood on the ice and watched the boat crumple and sink.

It didn't strike her, until all the excitement was over, that she was now stuck in the far south. She had no way to get back home. There was only forward into the snow.

So she picked up her sacks of food and walked toward the interesting lighted mound from yesterday, the glint of light that might be something or nothing.

THE SNOW WAS COLD, she knew, but she wasn't bothered by it. The wind, though—it blew sharp snowflakes into her face like pins and whipped her icy clothing against her in slaps. And underfoot, the snow's top layer of crust, ridged and sharpened by the wind, cut into her boots and feet. Every few dozen steps, she'd break through the crust to the soft fluffy snow underneath, plunging as far as her knee or even her thigh before catching herself with her other foot or her hands. She was sure there was ground somewhere underneath all this snow, but she only really knew this because she could see, at the top of some of the hills, bleak gray-brown rock, blown clean and bare. She hoped she could find the cave opening; she hoped it *was* a cave. She really, *really* hoped she could find trees. Something to build a new boat with, now that the sea had devoured her first one. Finding wood didn't seem likely, at least not anywhere near here. But who knew how far the land went?

Anyway, sulking wouldn't help anything. First things first. Find somewhere to get out of the wind. Somewhere to rest and store any food she might find (but what?).

Still running all these thoughts through her head, she struggled through the snow toward the lighted mound. As she got closer, it looked even more like a cave. She tried not to let her hopes get too high.

The sun was already setting. It had barely even risen above the rim of the horizon, and it was already going down. She hurried. She didn't want to sit out in the dark through the long night. Maybe she could build a snow fort. That might not be a bad idea. She'd look at the lighted hill and then build a snow shelter to crawl into and store her food. Sleep until morning.

She finally reached the lighted hill. And when she got to it, she saw that she'd hit some good luck. It *was* a cave—but a very strange cave.

Glowing faintly, a tunnel led into the hill and down. She peered as far as she could, but she couldn't see to the end of the passageway as it curved around. The source of the light was somewhere far ahead.

What was down there?

Rayel could see only two real options: the tunnel led to something good or to something dangerous. And if it was good, why not rush in? And if dangerous, why not rush as well? It had been weeks since Nunu left, months since she'd lost Solomon. She'd been alone for so long now that it was hard to comprehend what the danger might be. But surely—surely light meant something intelligent? Maybe even human?

Rayel stooped to enter the tunnel, which gradually descended. She walked a long time. The light source was always ahead of her, its glimmers refracting on the ice around her. The walls were made of ice, but the air seemed warm, and beneath her booted feet, the floor felt smooth like well-worn rock. She walked until she could no longer see her breath, and then the tunnel turned a sharp corner and opened. It opened out and out.

And it was glorious.

15

PUTNAM AND ARTIE. THE PRESENT.

*T*HEY SAILED south for several days almost without speaking. Artie didn't want to talk about the bears, and Putnam was irritated that she wouldn't. He admitted to himself that it might be petty to be mad at her—she was obviously used to keeping things to herself, obviously not used to treating anyone like a friend. But it stung that she wouldn't tell him more about it. After all, he was so easy to talk to! He was a good listener; he always nodded and said the right words in response. Also, he had agreed to run away from the island—even left behind her water sack that they so needed—hurrying away at Artie's insistence, and before seeing the bears.

When he saw them, he understood why Artie was so scared. But he also knew there was more to the story.

Artie said they chased her. But she refused to give any details. Where had she found them? How had she gotten away? Were there more than two? And . . . *bears?*

Bears, after all, didn't even *exist*. At least, not according to the stories he'd grown up on. They were like dragons or sea monsters: pretend. But these—these were definitely real. Or real-*ish*. He needed more explanation. He wanted to talk about them. And she was a boulder of silence.

ARTIE FELT RELIEVED: relieved to be away from the bears, and almost as relieved that Putnam was mad at her. If he stayed mad at her, she wouldn't have to talk with him. And Putnam, mad, was almost laughable. He didn't even yell or hit or *anything*. He just frowned deeply and grew quiet. She could handle that.

Of course, maybe he just hadn't lost his temper yet, and that was still coming. You never could tell.

She knew why he was angry; she wasn't stupid. He wanted her to talk, to explain everything about the island and what exactly had happened with the bears. But she just couldn't talk about it, how she stood in the bears' home, how she saw the hollows their bodies made in their beds, how they huffed as they followed her. If she put it all into words, the bears would seem even closer, their panting breaths even louder.

Besides, they were in the past now. No reason to remember them.

But though she put the bears out of her mind during the day, they inhabited her dreams. She found herself waking with a jerk several times every night, falling off cliffs trying to escape, or tripping over tree roots, or simply not running fast enough, their claws raking at her back. She'd yell or gasp as she flailed and fell through sleep to wake, dazed, in the cabin of the boat. And across from her, on the other side of the cabin with just the heater between them, she'd see Putnam's eyes, open in the darkness looking at her with concern. She'd duck and cocoon her head in her blanket and try to go back to sleep. But sleep was long in coming, and then another nightmare would jerk her out of it.

She only knew what bears were because of stories—stories from both the Islands and from Raftworld. But they were all *made-up* stories—no one thought bears were *real*. They were the bonfire stories that children listened to when they wanted to scare themselves—as they huddled under a blanket or cape with a grown-up who would protect them. The stories described the claws and teeth, the huge doglike shape, the long nose and small round ears, the white fur, and the padded feet as large as a person's head, with claws extending as long as your fingers. In some stories, the bears came into your house and stole your food and sat in your chairs and slept in your beds, like goblins. And in other stories, the bears lived in rough caves, and when you went near the caves, they came out and roared, like dragons. And like goblins and dragons, they were mythical.

And in none of the stories did their cave resemble the cozy home you always dreamed of having.

Artie knew now that bears were real. But one of the reasons to hold off from telling Putnam more about them was that somehow telling would *really* make them real. Right now she felt like she was keeping them, just barely, in the world of nightmares—and shutting them out of the daytime. Talking about them would make them daytime monsters, too.

PUTNAM, AS THE DAYS and—especially—nights went on, transformed from being angry to being worried. He could see Artie was having nightmares, and he could see she was scared. And that made him feel troubled for her, too. And not sure how to fix things.

He used to think he was good at fixing things—especially between people. But Artie refused to tell him, refused to let him make everything right again.

So they traveled on, barely speaking, through disturbed nights and anxious days.

Meanwhile, as days passed, the water grew choppier, filled with slush. Soon they began to see actual ice—slabs of it floating on the water and chunks sticking up that hinted at more ice beneath the surface—worrisome even to them with their shallow boat.

There wasn't much to do. Putnam took the sails down; they shouldn't move fast with so much ice around. He thought they would need to pole or paddle, but almost immediately they found a slow current that pulled them south, winding through the biggest chunks of ice either of them had ever seen—the *only* big chunks of ice Putnam had ever seen, actually. Artie's islands froze every year, but even she'd never seen this kind of winter. Where she lived, the sea stayed liquid away from shore; it only froze and cracked into a crust along its edges—the Island's shore. The giant mountains of ice that rose out of this ocean—well, this was a different world.

Putnam stood on deck with a pole to make sure that they didn't run into anything. Once in a while he stuck the pole out to push against a too-close slab of ice. But mostly he didn't have anything to do but shiver and daydream. When he got too cold, Artie would appear and take the pole from him. They traded spots all day long. At night they put the anchor down but stayed in the current so that the water wouldn't freeze around the boat. Artie explained—since Putnam had no experience with ice—that if they let the boat sit in still water, it would start to freeze and develop leaks. Could even break apart.

"I've seen it happen," she said. "My—someone—left a little rowboat in the water, anchored to the dock. And the ice wedged in and made cracks so that when spring came, the boat leaked like a basket." She shook her head, remembering. "So it'll be better if we keep the boat in the current."

"That makes sense," said Putnam. And the conversation for the day was over.

As they got farther from the bear island, Artie thought she'd sleep better. But she didn't. In fact, the nightmares got worse as they entered the ice fields. One morning—a week now since they'd left the island—she stood on the deck, pole in hand, and shaded her eyes to look far away, all around them. Ice and slushy water in front of them. Behind them, less ice, but just as much water. The island long out of sight.

But . . . there was something—on the horizon. She squinted. What was it?

Putnam came up to take his turn with the pole. "What are you looking at?" He shaded his eyes, too, then said, "There *is* something back there, isn't there?"

"It's nothing," said Artie. She looked again, and now she couldn't see anything, but horizon clear and bright. "Just ice."

"I guess so," agreed Putnam. "But wow, I could have sworn I saw an iceberg that was moving. I guess you get optical illusions when you're out here so long."

It wasn't an optical illusion. Artie had seen a chunk of ice lumbering toward them.

Like a giant bear. Like two bears walking on the water.

But that couldn't be.

ONE MORNING Putnam saw land: an island. Or something even bigger, and all made of ice and snow. It rose out of the ocean, grim and white and endless.

"Well," said Artie.

"Yep," said Putnam. "End of the road."

"You think it's here? What you're looking for?"

Putnam didn't know. He *felt* like there would be something here. The water was so briny that they could smell it all the time, and their clothes were covered in salt stains. The answer *had* to be here somewhere.

"Yes," he said.

She looked back at the horizon and then turned forward, shrugging. "Let's go take a look around."

But as Putnam and Artie poled through the ice toward shore, he couldn't shake the feeling of being followed. He kept looking over his shoulder. Whatever had happened to Artie on the island was starting to rub off on him now. He shook himself and straightened up. *Stop being afraid.* Artie might be falling apart since the bear island, but that meant it was up to him to hold everything together. To be the hero. To rescue them and save everyone.

He could have sworn, though, that when he'd studied the far distance where Artie had been looking, he'd seen two white bears, small and almost glowing against the bright horizon, riding a tiny raft. Following them.

16

RAYEL. ABOUT 100 YEARS EARLIER.

*T*HE FIRST thing Rayel did after she entered the giant cavern at the end of the ice tunnel was take off her boots. She stood on one leg at a time, unwilling to crouch or sit in this strange place, and freed first one foot, then the other. The ice under her soles felt warm, actually *warm*, like it wasn't ice at all. And the air around her glistened with moisture. She walked to the edge of the ice and stepped onto the rich, loamy earth. Far above, almost too high to make out, sunlight filtered through an enormous skylight of ice, and refracted and magnified, illuminating the entire cavern. It had been close to dusk when she entered the tunnel; somehow here it was still bright. Birds called and flew overhead; squirrel-like creatures chattered; leaves rustled.

Under the frozen south lay another world, a world of greenery and warmth. Small trees and bushes everywhere, with strange fruits that she'd never seen before. Birds entirely new to her, most of them multicolored and as bright as if dressed for one of her mother's parties. Lizards that changed color even as she stared at them.

She walked into the underground garden without thinking of danger—this was so clearly not an evil place. And if it was—well, then there wasn't anywhere in the world that was safe.

She walked for a good while, following what looked like a rough trail, before she came upon a stream—where she drank the coolest, purest water she'd ever tasted. As if all water began here, perhaps. And when she followed the stream toward its source, she began to hear, in the distance, the sound of crashing and splashing.

It was a waterfall. She saw it before she realized what it was—through the trees, water pouring down from a high ledge. When she turned the last bend of the faint path to see the cascade fully, she gasped in surprise—and not just because she'd never seen such a high waterfall before.

There was someone else there. A girl about her own age, maybe a little older. Sitting on a flat rock on the edge of the water, a rainbow behind her and mist hovering all around her. Weaving, on a small handloom, a long ribbon of bright fabric.

Of all things, weaving.

The girl looked up, all brown eyes and sun-filled skin. All

smile. All long thick black hair, except a small round bald spot on the top of her head, like someone had pressed a magic finger there. All bare feet and thick eyebrows and five scars down her shoulders disappearing into her shift, as if something had raked her back with sharp claws. All spark and light. She clicked her tongue against the roof of her mouth as she stood, and Rayel knew her.

"Hi," the girl said, biting off a long thread and holding up the finished ribbon. "I've been waiting for you."

17

PUTNAM AND ARTIE. THE PRESENT.

ARTIE AND Putnam had followed—without knowing it, of course, since Rayel had mostly disappeared long ago from the historical record—the same currents that Rayel had followed, and the currents had funneled them into the same stretch of icy land, where they'd climbed a hill just like Rayel had done, not the exact same hill but the next one over. And even though they arrived a hundred years after Rayel did, they found a similar icy landscape.

They had not, however, anchored their boat directly to an iceberg but had instead tied it *between* two icebergs and left it there, in the current, hoping to keep the hull from freezing. And they had bundled up before leaving the boat, because they didn't have Rayel's gifts with cold weather. They also didn't swim to shore from the boat—the water was too cold to do that—but had hung and swung, hand over hand, from the ropes they'd hitched to one of the icebergs. It was difficult, but safer than swimming.

On the boat there had been stowed a couple pairs of sun goggles which fisherfolk used on bright days on the water. Putnam and Artie wore them now to protect their eyes from the sun's glare on the snow. They both wore two layers of blanket-made capes, hooded, with the brims pulled low, and under that, all the rest of their clothing. Artie had fashioned boots, her first pair ever, from an old piece of tarp, and both wore extra socks and mittens made from a blanket. They had one walking stick that Putnam had brought from the boat tied to his back, which they shared. They had a small water sack tucked inside Artie's shirt to keep it from freezing, and a few pieces of dried food stored deep in Putnam's pockets. That was all.

They were not warm. Not even close.

Putnam wanted to find the source of the salt. Artie didn't believe they would find anything, but Putnam had gone ashore on the bear island when she wanted to, so she decided to do it here for him. Whatever they would find couldn't be worse than bears.

After they reached shore and climbed the long hill, they stood in the wind for a precious few moments trying to find a direction that looked promising. But there wasn't anything. Just endless snow.

Artie tried not to sound accusatory. "You said you'd find the problem. With the salty sea. Down here in the south." She definitely sounded accusatory. She stopped talking and shivered in silence. It wasn't like she had anywhere else to go. The only other island they'd found was inhabited by bears.

But she clearly couldn't live here, either.

PUTNAM COULD hear the tone in Artie's voice. And part of him agreed with it. What had he been thinking? That he would get here and magically figure something out? That saving the world would be *easy*? This deep southern island looked endless. And formless. White everywhere. No trees, no plants, no animals, no birds. Nothing to keep them alive. And nothing to suggest what was turning the sea to salt.

He wasn't sure what he'd expected. A salt-making windup machine, cranking away? An evil wizard casting spells? A giant sled made of salt, crashed from the heavens? Maybe there was some clue farther ahead . . . ?

Artie nudged him, and he looked at her, then realized she was shivering, not trying to poke at him. They needed to find shelter or get back to the boat. Or at least get off this windy hill. Make a new plan.

He pointed back toward the boat, and she nodded and started down the slippery slope they'd just climbed.

Before Putnam followed her, he looked around one last time and then toward the sea, over Artie's head. There was the ocean again, cold but somehow still more friendly than the frozen ground. And there was the boat, bobbing in the water, and there—

He gasped.

No.

Artie saw them the same time he did. She stiffened and jerked back so quickly that she fell on her butt. Then she turned to Putnam, her face in a grimace of terror.

Two bears were standing on shore looking up, up, up at them. Putnam's well-made raft bobbed in the water behind them.

The bears lowered their heads and began walking up the hill.

ARTIE AND Putnam raced down the far side of the hill, a long, slow slope that seemed to head off into an abyss of whiteness. There was nowhere else to run; the bears had blocked their way back to the boat.

But even as they ran, they both knew escape was hopeless. The bears would catch them: there was nowhere for them to hide in all this whiteness. For a desperate moment Putnam imagined digging a hole in the snow and burying himself in it, but there was no time. No time.

They threw themselves to their chests and sledded down the hill on their blanket capes. This sledding was painful—there were shards and bumps and jagged slashes in the snow crust all the way down. Next to him, Artie bumped her face on the snow, hard, and yelped. They kept sliding.

At the bottom they jumped up.

"Your chin," said Putnam.

She swiped with her makeshift mitten; it came away with blood.

"There," said Putnam. He pointed upward and stared, mesmerized. The bears had reached the top of the hill, where they themselves had stood only moments earlier. One creature plopped onto its stomach like a dog, as if tired from climbing. The other lifted its nose in the air and sniffed.

"Let's go," gasped Putnam. The air was so cold, it bit into his lungs like a knife. *Like a claw*, he thought, and he grabbed Artie's hand and yanked her into motion.

They ran as hard and fast as they could, stumbling often in the sharp crusty snow and holding hands to keep each other up. But where could they go? It was hopeless.

Putnam could feel Artie starting to lag, her breath becoming more and more ragged. And he could feel it in himself, too. They couldn't run forever. He glanced back over his shoulder. The hilltop was empty. Where were the bears? It would be impossible to see the bears, white against white, until the monsters were right on top of them. Artie and Putnam, on the other hand, glowed bright in their blanket capes against the snow. Like targets.

Keep running.

As Artie stumbled, Putnam yanked and pulled her forward. Then Artie pointed slightly off to the side, panting. Putnam veered the way she was pointing, dragging her along. But really, what difference did it make which direction they went? Or did she see something he did not? He squinted through his sun goggles as they staggered ahead.

Then he saw it too: a lighted patch of snow. The sun was beginning to set, and as the daylight faded, a round spot in the snow—not that far ahead of them, it seemed—glowed bright.

Whatever it was, it was something to run toward. Maybe, just maybe, it would be something—what?—that could help them.

MEANWHILE, ARTIE knew—she knew—it was some kind of hole in the ground. She didn't know how she knew this, but something inside her understood. This would be a place of safety. Sanctuary. It glowed in the fading light like a holy place.

She could also hear, through and underneath the gasping of herself and Putnam, the bears drawing closer. She could feel her hair rise on the back of her neck like someone was breathing on it. There was nothing for it but to run, as fast as they could, and hope to make it. There was no way to stand and fight. She plunged ahead.

The glowing thing *was* a hole in the ground. They could both see it now, a lighted tunnel only a few steps ahead of them. So close. And big enough for them to slide into, one at a time, quick as quick.

Then Putnam stumbled, his foot plunging through the crust, and he flew forward onto his face, dragging Artie down with him.

She scrambled up, but Putnam didn't move, even when she yanked his arm, hard. She screamed and tugged with all her might, pulling him forward and dislodging his foot from the snow. Slowly he rose, wavering unsteadily, his face now bloody like hers.

"We gotta *move*," she gasped. "Now." Her lungs were being squeezed by a giant icy hand.

He nodded, then looked back again.

Artie looked at the same time, and everything in her froze: her blood, her brain, her heart, all of it.

The bears stood only a few yards away from them.

They all stared, Artie and Putnam gasping for breath, shoulders heaving and bloody faces, the bears with hungry looks on their faces, bright-eyed and excited, not tired at all.

Then Putnam thrust back his shoulders and straightened out, and at the same moment, the bigger of the two bears stood on its hind legs, so enormous and so close.

PUTNAM'S MIND felt suddenly clear. *This is what I am meant to do. This is how I save Artie. Not the whole world. Artie.*

He pushed Artie behind him and held his walking stick like a spear. "Get to the tunnel," he said, "and I'll follow."

ARTIE DIDN'T understand. *Couldn't* understand. Was he going to fight the bears?

"I'll buy you time. Then I'll run, too," said Putnam. "GO!"

The second bear rose up on its hind legs like the first. Both beasts roared. There was nothing but roaring.

And suddenly Artie couldn't think anything except, *RUN*. She turned and sprinted, leaving Putnam behind to die, the roaring and screaming behind her filling her ears.

PART TWO

How the Sea Turned to Salt

RAYEL AND UNA, ABOUT 100 YEARS EARLIER.

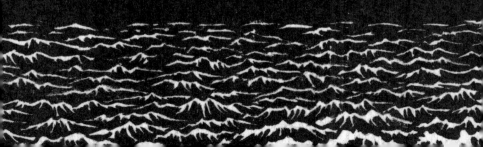

*T*HERE IS maybe nothing better than traveling to the bottom of the world and finding a friend you thought you'd lost forever. Rayel thought her heart might burst.

The girl in the cavern at the bottom of the world denied that her name was Nunu and claimed she had no memory of being a dolphin; that, she said, was crazy talk. She seemed really not to understand what Rayel was talking about. But she knew Rayel and her history, and she'd been waiting for Rayel to arrive. Her name, she said, was Una.

"Okay," said Rayel. Nunu—*Una*—wouldn't lie. Who knows, maybe that was how the magic worked for her. And it was wonderful that they could now talk to each other in the same language. Una and Rayel spent all of that first day together, and the second and the third, and so on. Rayel told Una about the rest of her journey and how she arrived to the underground world. Una told about the cavern, which she'd had some time to explore. But for her it was as though nothing existed before this underground world. About her original family she'd only say that they'd been lost at sea. She hadn't seen them since she was very young, almost a baby. She couldn't remember more.

Una swam for hours every day in the stream and water-fall and ate only fish. She said she'd eaten fish for so long she couldn't change her ways, not even now that she was living where there were delicious plants. When she wasn't swimming, she would sit near the water and weave on the loom she'd built for herself out of sticks. She wove delicate grasses into mats they could sleep on and flax-like strands into clothes they could wear. The soft tassels of grain she wove into hair ribbons and bracelets. She spent long hours braiding Rayel's hair.

Rayel learned that although she didn't feel the cold, Una did. Una couldn't—wouldn't—go to the surface of the deep south, instead shivering and shaking her head whenever Rayel suggested exploring there.

They didn't need to go up, anyway. Their underground world had everything these two could need for life: fruits and vegetables and birds' eggs for Rayel; warm air for Una; fish for both of them; sunlight somehow brighter than on the surface and refracted through a roof so high above that it looked like sky; drizzles of rain that fell every morning from the conden-sation on the high ceiling; rich dirt and soft grass and running water so pure it was like nothing Rayel had ever tasted before.

This underground cavern had everything one might need to survive. Except one thing: adventure.

ONE DAY as they were sitting on the bank of the stream, Una still dripping from a swim and Rayel cleaning carrots and potatoes in the river before cooking them for her dinner, she finally got up the courage to ask Una how she came to get her scars. Rayel had seen them again when Una was swimming—deep crevasses down her back, healed but still ridged and angry-looking. Welts that would never go away. The same as Nunu's.

Una smiled. "We all have scars." Her teeth shone in the dusk; so did the little bald spot on her head, the blowhole mark, more noticeable when her thick hair was wet.

"Not what I meant," said Rayel.

The other girl tossed her head and laughed. "I know." She lay back on the grass, her hands clasped under her head and her elbows out to the side like fins. "It happened before I came here. I . . . think I went to an island." She shook her head. "My memory isn't too good."

"By yourself?"

"After I lost my family. I think."

Rayel waited, but Una didn't say more. "What island?"

"I don't know its name. It was crescent-shaped. The bay was warm because a hot spring fed into it. Oh, there were so many fish." She smacked her lips at the memory, then shivered.

"What happened?" Rayel sat above her friend, the washed carrots and potatoes forgotten on the grass between them.

"What made the scars?" *And was that the same island that Nunu and I visited . . . ?*

"I didn't look carefully. I just swam into the shallow water in the bay, not really paying attention, you know? I'd just lost my family. I was there but not there?"

Rayel waited, tapping at the bump on her head until Una reached up and took her hand.

"It was in the bay, standing in the water. Maybe It was fishing. Seemed like It was waiting for me. It grabbed me with its terrible claws. I just barely got away, trailing blood after me."

Rayel could hardly breathe. "What . . . was . . . it?"

Una looked surprised—surprised Rayel didn't know, maybe also surprised that she was still there, listening. She dropped Rayel's hand.

"Don't you know? Haven't you been there?"

"To that island? But I—I didn't see anything."

"It was a bear. Turns out they're as real as me." More to herself she added, "There was only one then. But later, there were two. Why two? One for each of us? One for everyone who lands there?"

Rayel shook her head. Una wasn't making sense.

They both lay on their backs for a long time and watched the stars that were coming out overhead—or, not stars but whatever they were, glittering on the ceiling of whatever it was up there. The lid of their world. The entire cavern still glowed gently with stored light.

"So, how did you . . . get better?" Rayel couldn't quite say *heal*.

Una just turned her had and looked at Rayel. She didn't speak, but Rayel could see the words in her eyes. *You.*

RAYEL WAS UNDERGROUND with Una for the better part of a year, turning fifteen in this paradise. Every day was warm and perfect. Yet Rayel felt the smallness of this enclosed world. It was like she was tucked inside someone's pocket—but what had at first felt safe and cozy now felt like a prison. She missed the ocean and living on a raft. Out in the open. And she missed adventure.

Una, too, seemed ready to leave, finally. She talked about the ocean with a deep longing. When Rayel told her about Raftworld, she said it sounded wonderful, and when Rayel went back, she would go with her and live there, too—or if not on Raftworld, then at least near it. Rayel smiled at the other girl's murky way of speaking. But whether Una lived on the giant raft or in the water near it, she'd be close. Rayel would have a friend nearby.

Rayel had been gone long enough. Her fiancé had surely married someone else by now. Even if he hadn't, though, she knew now that she could stand up to him and to her parents—appeal to the council if she needed to, and explain what she'd overheard and why she didn't want to marry this man. If that didn't work—well, she could run away again. She knew she could, because she'd already done it. And she'd have her friend.

But there was still so much here, in the frozen south, to see. Before she went back to Raftworld, she wanted to explore *this* world more. After all, she'd made it all the way to the cold lands, something no other Raftworlder had ever done, and she had the magic gift to survive here. So why not return as the first human who'd explored the entire south? Maybe there was more to find before leaving: more underground caverns, maybe even habitable land above ground if one traveled far enough. Who knew when Raftworld might want a permanent place to settle? And if they ever did, she'd be the hero who had found it.

Una was excited to go to Raftworld. She'd begun weaving warmer clothing so that she could survive the walk to the ocean and the days and weeks at sea. Rayel began building a raft they could lug out of this place in pieces and put together at the water, a raft with a small cabin for Una to stay out of the cold.

But all the while they were building and weaving, Rayel kept thinking about the frozen land around them. And finally one day she said what she was thinking, even though it would make Una unhappy. "Before we go, I'd like to walk around outside for a while."

"Underground is nice," said Una. "Warm."

"But we don't know what's out there," said Rayel. "Not all of it. There could be more places like this cavern. Or *better* places. We'll just go look. Then we'll go to Raftworld."

Finally, reluctantly, Una agreed: as soon as she'd woven enough cloth to make a warm outfit for herself, they'd explore.

Another month passed, and finally Una's snow outfit was ready. By that time, Rayel had finished the little raft with the cabin—it sat in several pieces on the ground near the waterfall—and she was so bored she was almost ready to climb the walls of the sunny cave. It was all so perfect and so still and so aggravating. She wanted wind, and shifting ocean, and the feeling of cold weather looking for her and not finding her.

It was just past the height of summer, or what passed for the height of summer in the deep south, when they stepped outside. The sun shone almost all day long, setting for only a few hours each night. The brightness felt like life to Rayel. For though she could not feel cold, she could feel heat, and she realized she hadn't felt direct sunlight in a long time.

The two girls took turns pulling a sled filled with items they would need: fresh-caught fish for Una; dried food for Rayel; a change of clothes in case Una's clothing became wet; a little tent for Una to keep warm in (there was room for Rayel in the tent, too, but she didn't *need* it); and a little stove with a pile of wood scraps, for Una. Most of the sled, in fact, carried sticks for burning.

On their backs the girls wore cloaks that Una had made. Rayel wore one, too, but only because her friend had made it; she planned to give it to Una if Una got too cold in only her own cloak. And they'd fashioned visors from tinted gypsum, to protect their eyes from the bright glare; it was impossible to see without the visors pulled down over their faces.

Even through all those layers, Rayel could feel fingers of sunlight tickling her head and shoulders. She loosened her cloak.

Una, meanwhile, pulled hers tighter and hunched against the wind, shivering. "How long are we going to stay out here?"

"We've just started," said Rayel. "And you'll warm up when we walk. I promise."

Una nodded, willing to try, and they set off inland, away from where Rayel's boat had sunk, toward a slight rise in the land.

A couple of hours later, the slight rise in the land was closer, and it was more than a slight rise. A mountain? Distances and heights were hard to judge here. But it looked rocky as they got closer to it, and Rayel thought it would be a good place to look for more underground land—or even just normal, nonmagical snow caves—and for any other signs of life. She gestured toward it. "Let's get as far as we can and then set up camp for the night."

Una rubbed her mittened fingers together and stuffed them under her armpits. "I don't know if I can make it that far. My feet are getting really cold. Sore. I don't want frostbite."

Rayel tried to imagine what frostbite would feel like. Such a strange word.

Looking up at Rayel, Una explained: the tingling in the fingers and toes, then the numbness and clumsiness. If you stayed out long enough, the eventual death from cold.

Rayel listened, though it was all just words to her. She couldn't *feel* it. "I believe you. Should we stop now? For the night?"

Una nodded, relieved. "I just need to warm up."

They set up the tent, and Una crawled inside with the stove, lit a piece of wood from the small stock they'd brought along, and huddled over it. Rayel crawled inside, and they shared a lunch and rested. A couple of hours later, they started up again.

They walked for two days, zigzagging away from their cavern, stopping often to warm up and nap, traveling toward the mountain and then climbing the mountain.

Although they could see far into the distance from its smooth, windblown summit, they didn't spot any entrances to underground caverns, and they couldn't see any trees or grass or anything alive. They'd discovered frozen land and snow that seemed to go on forever.

Una was cold all the time now—and more and more uneasy the farther they got from the ocean. At the top of the low mountain, she pivoted slowly, scanning the horizon for water. There was none in sight. "Can we go back?"

"We still have enough food and wood to go a bit farther. Maybe that next mountain." Rayel pointed into the distance. "Then we'll go back. I promise." She felt sure there had to be more to this southern world. There was the magic already of her gift with cold, and the astounding underground cave, and the presence of Una herself . . .

It was hard to even imagine her as Nunu anymore. The transformation was so believable.

As if she knew what Rayel was thinking, Una said, "I think the world gets wilder and more magical the farther south you go. That's my theory. Everything's more intense here, so the magic is, too." Then she sighed. "But I don't think there's more to this land. I think we've already found all the enchantment here."

Rayel nodded. Una was probably right about the magic being stronger in the south. After all, here was where she had found a home where she was solely loved. That was magic, too.

As soon as Rayel had that idea, she thought, *Solomon*. And memories from her old life—mostly memories about her little brother—flooded back. Things she had tried not to think about too much since she'd left home. So many things she missed about him. His warm skin, smooth under her hand when she touched his cheek. The feel of his head brushing against her arm when he snuggled up to her. His quick smile. The way he laughed when he beat her at games—and the way he laughed even more when she beat him. His head bent over a book and his light, high voice slowly making out the words. The way his nose wrinkled when their mom said something unkind to anyone (especially his sister). The way he ran across the docks when it was time to go boating, a flock of boys and girls running along with him.

She missed him. Even on the other side of the world, she'd

never stop missing him. She understood this better now than when she had left Raftworld. She'd always missed having parents who loved her, and she'd thought Solomon made up for that. But he didn't; his death taught her about different kinds of sadness. The pain of losing Solomon was staggering. But somehow the pain of losing love she'd never had was almost worse. It would always be an ugly scar. How could she go back?

"We should stay here," she said. The words fell out of her mouth unplanned. "Not *here*, not in the snow. But in the cavern. I'll go out and explore sometimes on my own, and you won't even have to go out in the cold, and we'll live in the cavern together, and it'll be safe, and we'll be happy."

Una stared at her. "You *promised*." There was real anger in her voice—and coldness, too. She turned and walked down the mountain, pulling the sled behind her, toward the warm cavern.

Rayel sighed. She'd messed up. But she didn't understand why it was such a big deal to Una—it wasn't like Raftworld was her home, or even like she remembered her original home.

She was, after all, a dolphin.

Una was a small figure partway down the mountain. It was amazing how quickly she could move when she was angry.

Before Rayel followed, she looked around one last time, hoping to see something. Something amazing.

And she did. Far off in the distance, she saw what looked like two . . . What *were* they? Large white creatures, almost the same shade as the snow, made visible by their blue shadows. Lumbering across the ice. So far away they looked almost like toys. They looked exactly like the way bears had been described in the stories she'd heard when she was little.

Two of them—like Una had said. One for each.

She shook her head, and suddenly they were gone, merged back into the landscape. Or maybe imagined in the first place.

Rayel turned and followed Una home. She wouldn't mention the bears—if that was what they were.

IT TOOK them only a long day to get back to the underground world. Rayel trailed behind as Una stormed ahead, refusing to stop for any amount of cold, determined to get back.

In the cavern, Una dove into the stream and swam for a long hour while Rayel unpacked the sled, parked now next to the raft pieces. When Una finally emerged from the water and shook herself off, Rayel said, "I'm sorry. But it's the truth. I don't want to go back. Not yet. Maybe not ever. It—it wasn't a good place for me."

"But I'll be there with you," Una said, "and it will be better. And I want to go. I need more people than what we have here. Maybe a boyfriend someday, maybe children someday, definitely more friends. I was never meant to be alone. I belong in a group."

"So I'm not good enough for you."

"That's not fair! I didn't say I was going to get rid of you. I just need other friends, *too*. And I'm trapped here—I can't explore,

I can't go anywhere—because of the cold. You don't know how that feels."

"I know what it's like to be trapped." Rayel glowered. "I was stuck on Raftworld. Besides," she said, "I think my vote counts more. It was my home, not yours."

Una flinched as if she'd been slapped. She straightened and said in a low voice, "I thought our votes were both worth the same." Her eyes darkened even more than usual, the two dots in them glinting like double pupils. "You think I don't matter as much as you."

"I never said that! I just don't want to go back. Not now."

"And maybe not ever."

Rayel nodded, relieved. Una understood. Una always understood. She had come to the deep south for Rayel, after all.

Una stared her in the face for a full minute. It seemed like forever. "Selfish," she said.

Then she turned and dove into the stream, swimming away from the water fall and downstream, toward the hard gypsum walls of the cavern. Rayel ran along the bank calling after her, but Una's head never came above the water; she never heard Rayel—or if she did, she was too angry or hurt to listen. She swam all the way to where the stream ran into a crevasse in the cavern wall on its way to the sea, and she swam into the crevasse. She disappeared.

RAYEL WAITED at the crevasse for hours, but Una never came back.

She returned to the waterfall, and there she cried. For Solomon. For Nunu. Most of all, now, for Una. For all the mistakes she'd made and the awful thing she'd said. The awful thing she'd thought. How could she think someone else wasn't as important as she was? That her needs outweighed theirs?

Finally, she cried for herself, because she could see a pattern now, a pattern of herself losing those she loved, a pattern of grief tracing itself out over and over again, like a child practicing rowing: circle and pull, circle and pull, circle and pull, all the motions connected, on and on in an endless invisible chain across the wide sea.

As she cried, she hardened. There is no other way to describe it. She felt like the cold had finally found her and she was turning to ice, or maybe to stone. She wasn't sure. She cried for hours, standing on the edge of the water, stiff and unmoving. Then something happened.

Something arrived.

A bear. She saw it out of the corner of her eye. One bear. Where did the other go? *One for each of us. One for everyone who lands there.* Had the other one followed Una, and was this one hers?

The bear approached her slowly, sniffing and growling. It was enormous.

Something snapped inside Rayel. The bear wasn't scared of her *at all*. It made her so angry. She didn't move. She kept crying, tears running down her face and neck. The bear swiped at her one time, raking its claws across her stone-hard arm and then whimpering when its claws were damaged. She felt a rush of power. Her arm didn't even bleed.

And with a mighty effort, she moved her almost-frozen body, and she grabbed the bear and held on. This bear was *hers*.

LATER, IT was just Rayel again, on the bank of the stream. She stood next to the waterfall, in the shade of the tall tree, and she cried. For what she'd done to the bear. For how it made her feel inside. And for everything and everyone she'd lost, including herself.

She hardened even more. She remembered how Una had tried to describe frostbite. But this wasn't freezing, which begins in your fingers and toes and your nose and cheeks and slowly moves from these outposts to your limbs, and only after your limbs surrender does it invade your internal organs and your brain. No, when Rayel hardened, it was something that happened from the inside out. First, all hunger disappeared. Then her heart and lungs slowed down, finally solidifying like granite. Then her brain felt heavy and slow, and her thoughts calcified (*gone, gone, gone,* their final and repeating word). Lastly—though it all happened quickly at this point—her body petrified in place, statued under the tree next to the river.

The only thing that did not freeze?

Her eyes.

Or more correctly, her tear ducts, which continued to produce tears. The tears ran down her hardened form and slid off her toes into the stream. The stream ran down into an underground river.

The river carried the tears all the way to the sea. A constant current of tears. And over the long years, those tears altered the enormous ocean.

Rayel's tears.

The salty sea.

PART THREE

The Bears of the Southern Sea

1

PUTNAM AND ARTIE.

*P*UTNAM STOOD on the snow just a few steps from the tunnel, walking stick in hand, the bears rearing above him. When they roared, he screamed at them and jabbed the stick forward. He did not feel brave. He knew he would die when they attacked. But he didn't know what else to do.

He tried to *sound* brave. He tried to sound like he had a trick up his sleeve, like maybe he had some magic that would suddenly transform him into something even bigger and scarier than a bear. And who knew? Maybe he did. Maybe there was something special in him that would reveal itself now, when he needed it most.

But of course that was wishful thinking. He screamed as loud as he could manage, and he jabbed his walking stick, and he didn't transform even the tiniest bit, and the bears didn't look at all impressed. They slapped back down to all fours and glared at him. One of them licked its chops. Then they sauntered toward him.

It was almost insulting how they didn't even run at him. Like they knew he couldn't escape.

Despairing, Putnam hurled the stick like a javelin. It hit the closest bear in the face, just above the eye, and the bear's head jerked back as if a small bird had struck him. Then it shook its head slowly and sauntered forward again.

Putnam turned and ran.

No, he didn't *run*. He practically flew. He didn't even draw breath; there wasn't time. He plunged away from the bears, toward the hole, blindly hoping to get there before they reached him.

When a bear raked its claws across his back, Putnam didn't feel pain, not exactly. He knew what was happening immediately. The sharp burning slash pulled a cry out of him in a voice that didn't even sound like his own. He stumbled. Fell to his hands and knees. Felt his body give up.

There was a next blow coming. He knew it.

He couldn't look back, but he knew they were there; he knew they were waiting for him to turn his head so they could kill him as they looked into his eyes.

He knew.

Slowly, he turned his head.

And at that moment, his hands were gripped in a fierce vise, and he was dragged forward, faster than he could imagine, into the tunnel.

ARTIE HAD run to the tunnel almost without thinking, the screaming and roaring propelling her forward like a bird blown by a hurricane. But the jarring drop into the tunnel shook her breath out of her, and she was able to make her feet stop, force herself to pause.

Putnam.

The entrance to the tunnel had plunged down several feet to a small ledge—she was now perched on it—and then there was a steep downward slope. If she'd taken even one more step forward she'd have hurtled into a narrow tube, a smooth slide that appeared to go downward forever. Who knew where it ended up? And she'd have been gone, unable to help Putnam at all.

As it was, she needed to do something.

He'd saved her.

No one had ever saved her before.

Now she needed to save him.

But she'd never saved anyone. She had no idea how to do it. Or if she could.

Artie poked her head out of the ground just in time to see Putnam, only an arm's length away, wheezing, on his hands and knees. His head slowly turned away from her to look back at the bears, who were *right there* above them. One had a claw raised as if it had just swiped at Putnam—or was about to.

No time. Move. She grabbed Putnam's wrists and yanked as hard as she could, falling back into the hole as she did and slamming into the little ledge again. Putnam lay on top of her, a dead weight. Was he breathing?

He was, but he wasn't moving. It was like he'd . . . collapsed. Her hands wrapped around. His back felt sticky.

Above her the light from the tunnel opening suddenly eclipsed. Lying under Putnam's body, looking up, she saw a terrifying white head poke into the tunnel, sniff its long nose, and pull back. Then, slowly, a powerful front leg reached in, five long claws extended. The paw drew nearer, stirring in the air like it was trying to scoop out the last delicious filling from a jar. She watched in terror.

When the claw, circling and slowly descending, had almost reached Putnam's back, Artie jerked into motion. They had no choice. The bears would pull them out onto the surface. Would kill them. She rolled Putnam over in her arms so that he faced outward, his back pressed against her stomach.

And she shoved herself and him feetfirst down the slide. Into the unknown. Into adventure or death or maybe just nothingness.

Away from the bears.

There was, she knew as they hurtled down the smooth icy tube, no way back.

2

ARTIE AND PUTNAM.

*A*S SHE shot down the long slide into darkness, Artie wished desperately that she had free hands. Not that she could have slowed herself down—there was nothing to grab onto; the slide was made of perfectly smooth ice, as if it had been built just for them to hurtle down at top speed. But if her hands had been free, she could have at least put them out to cushion the ride. As it was, she clutched Putnam, unconscious in her arms, to her chest and wrapped her legs around him, and she cushioned *his* ride while her shoulders, knees, ankles, and spine banged into solid ice over and over again. She tucked her head forward into Putnam's shoulder and managed to keep most of the blows on her body instead of her head, but that was all she was able to do. If she survived, she'd be a mass of bruises.

The ride seemed to go on forever, though it was really less

than a minute. Long enough to be terrifying. The tunnel grew darker and darker, and they flew faster and faster, until she *knew* they would land somewhere in a crunch of bones on ice and die.

But that didn't happen. Instead, the slope flattened, and their hurtling downward slowed until finally they were sliding forward, not down, gradually slowing as you would at the bottom of a long, steep hill on a sled in winter.

Putnam never reacted. He jostled around in her arms as they swerved down the tunnel, but he didn't move on his own. Was he even still breathing?

When they stopped sliding, they sat in a darkness so intense that Artie wouldn't have known Putnam was there if she hadn't been holding him. She leaned forward, her cheek against his, hoping he was still breathing.

Yes. The silence here was so deep, she could hear his light intake of air, the small sigh escaping from his mouth.

Gently she disentangled herself from him. The tunnel had broadened out; she couldn't quite stand (as she found when she reached up to feel the ceiling), but she could stoop over Putnam and lay him down. She turned him on his side and felt his back. Still wet and sticky—as were her chest and stomach where he had been pressed against her on the slide. Blood. She knew what blood felt like in the dark: warm and tacky. Carefully she felt his whole back. His clothes were shredded, and so was his skin, with five long, deep cuts. The cuts were oozing rather than spurting, so that was good. But he'd lost a lot of blood. That was less good.

She removed her outer cloak, shivering. They each had an outer and an inner cloak—really just two blankets they'd cut to fit over their heads. Putnam's were no good anymore, hanging in bloody strips, though the hood part still seemed okay, so she left it and simply wrapped her blanket tightly around his back and shoulders, slipping it under him and tying it around his stomach like a giant bandage.

Putnam lay on his side, and though she couldn't see him in the dark, she knew he was still unconscious. She moved around to his face and flicked it gently. "Wake up."

He didn't wake up.

She talked to him for a few minutes, reminding him who he was and telling him where they were. His eyes remained shut, and his face, growing barely visible as her eyes slowly adjusted to the dark, looked restful and at peace. She almost hated to wake him. But they couldn't stay here. Here was nowhere. And the ice was cold, seeping into her bones as she sat on it. Her whole body felt like a giant shiver.

Finally she slapped his face—not hard, but hard enough to sting—and he opened his eyes, groaning as he did.

"Are you okay?" asked Artie. What a dumb question. Of course he wasn't okay.

"What happened?"

"The bears—" said Artie. She stopped herself, because Putnam's face immediately changed.

"Right," he said, wincing. "I remember."

"We got away," Artie said. "But we're kind of . . . well, we're way underground and lost."

She gestured around them into the darkness.

"Can we go back? When the bears are gone, I mean?" He curled a little tighter on his side, like his body didn't want to get up.

"No."

He didn't question her, just accepted her answer. "Well, then I guess . . ." He thought.

"It's a tunnel," said Artie. "I think."

"Tunnels go somewhere," said Putnam.

"Okay," said Artie. Putnam was suggesting that they follow the path, and honestly, she couldn't see any other option. "Can you get up?"

"Sure," he said. He pushed himself to one elbow and gasped. "Maybe not."

"Can I—can I help you?"

"Give me a second."

They sat in silence. Artie looked around and realized the

darkness she'd thought was so deep wasn't actually complete. Ahead of them, away from the slide they'd shot down, the tunnel glowed faintly. Maybe—odd to think so, so far underground—maybe there was a way out. She could hope.

"You saved me from the bears," said Putnam. "You came back for me and pulled me into the tunnel. Didn't you?"

"I ran away first."

"I told you to! You came back. For me."

She nodded and then realized he might not see her. "But only after you saved me. And I was going to keep running, but you yelled really loud. And I couldn't . . ." She couldn't even say everything she wanted to say. He'd offered up his life to save hers. No one had ever done that before. Probably no one ever would again. It was the kind of thing that happened once in a lifetime, if ever. It was a crazy thing to do. *He* was crazy.

"You came back," said Putnam. "We saved each other. That's what friends do, right?"

"We're friends?" she asked. The question popped out before she thought about how rude it might sound.

"Of course," said Putnam.

It was really cold in the tunnel. Artie's eyes felt funny, like ice was melting in them. Or water was freezing in them, she wasn't quite sure. "Can you get up now?"

"Help me?"

She pulled his hand, and they both stood, stooping in the low tunnel. Putnam swayed, and Artie slipped under one shoulder to support him. Carefully they shuffled along the slick tunnel, hobbling and slipping toward the dim light.

PUTNAM COULD feel everything. For a little while, even after he woke up, the pain wasn't too bad: a heat on his back like a bad sunburn. But now there were knives plunged into his back, sharp lines of fire running down his spine. His face hurt, too—probably from smashing into the ice when Artie had first pulled him into the tunnel—and his shoulders ached as if they'd been jerked almost out of their sockets, and the backs of his legs were bruised from the trip down the chute. But more than anything, his back was aflame.

He groaned as they shuffled down the tunnel; every tiny slip on the ice was excruciating.

"Does it hurt?" said Artie. Which was almost the worst question she could have asked.

"A bit," said Putnam, which was almost the worst answer. He tried again. "It's burning."

"Would it help to lie on the ice for a few minutes?"

"I don't think it's that kind of burning."

They seemed to walk down the tunnel forever. They stopped to rest several times, whenever Putnam began to stumble and lean too heavily on Artie and Artie began to stagger under Putnam's weight. Putnam's mouth turned cottony with thirst, and when Artie spoke, her voice sounded dry and tight. They'd long ago emptied the water bag slung around Artie's neck.

The light in the tunnel continued to glow, but it never seemed to grow brighter. The light's source was always farther down, around the next corner, out of sight.

What was the point of continuing? For the first time in his life, Putnam understood how a person could simply give up: you'd give up because there was no reason to go on, no end to the tunnel. You'd give up not because you'd *reached* the light, but because you'd finally realized you never would.

The next time they sat down to rest, Putnam sank onto the ice and let its cold seep into his legs. And when Artie said it was time to get up and move on, he shook his head no.

"You need more rest?" she asked. Her voice was scratchy. "We can stay a little longer, but then we should move on."

"No."

"I've lived through a lot of winters, and I have to tell you that if we stay in one spot too long, the cold will get to us and we'll die. We have to keep moving."

"No."

She glared at him in the dim light. "No?"

"I'm going to stay here. You can go on. But there isn't any point. We're going to die anyway. So I'll stay here."

"*I'm* not going to die."

"We're both going to die. This tunnel doesn't go anywhere. We're underground at the far south of the world, and no one is going to rescue us, and we're going to die."

"Get up!" She stood, hands on hips, glaring. The tunnel had broadened sometime during their trek, and now they could both stand upright—if Putnam stood. "Are you getting up?"

"No. I'm going to die here."

"You are so *stupid!*" Artie stomped her feet, which made Putnam smile. "This isn't funny!"

"I'm staying here."

"*Fine!* I'm going."

And that was it.

Artie marched away down the tunnel, walking much faster now that she didn't have his weight to half carry. The tunnel curved slightly, and after a moment she disappeared.

She was gone.

Putnam's back hurt too much to lean against the tunnel wall. He lay down on his side, facing the tunnel end where Artie had disappeared, and gazed into the glowing half-light. The cold slithered up into his body from the ice floor, but it didn't feel *quite* as cold as it had at their last stop. He took off his mitten and laid his hand on the ice. It was true: the ice felt warmer, less like ice and more like stone. That probably meant he was close to freezing. He'd heard stories. It was weird but true that you'd feel warmer the closer you grew to turning to ice yourself. Maybe it was your body's way of becoming one with its surroundings. He closed his eyes.

He might have dozed off; he wasn't sure how long Artie had been gone. The time seemed both long and short. When he opened his eyes, the side of his face was pressed against the ice, which felt cool but not cold. Artie stood in front of him, hands on hips again.

He was hallucinating. Maybe this was something that happened before you died of hypothermia: you saw things that weren't there?

But why did he see *Artie*? Why not his dad, or—or even his mom, who'd been gone so long that she might as well have died, too? Or he could have seen any of his schoolmates from Raftworld. Or maybe he could have seen an ocean again; he loved the ocean. But no: here in a hallucination that could be literally *anything*, here was Artie and the endless tunnel. Just like in real life.

"You are such a jerk," said Artie.

He lifted his head. "Am—am I dead?"

"Shut up, okay?"

"Dreaming?"

"Yeah," she said sarcastically. "We're still on the boat. The whole thing with the bears was just a fantasy." She snapped her fingers in his face. "Wake up."

"My back is killing me."

"Well, then I guess it's not a dream. Now get your butt up and start walking."

"You don't need to be mean." Putnam sat up.

"I'm not leaving you here. You jerk. Get up."

Slowly he stood, swaying. He didn't feel any better than he had before she'd stormed off, but he didn't have the energy to argue. In fact, he had no energy at all. "I don't think I . . ." He stumbled against her, and she caught his shoulders.

For a moment she stared into his face as if she had no idea what to do. She looked scared more than angry. He wanted to tell her that she shouldn't be frightened, that the ice didn't even feel cold anymore and it would all be okay. But the words wouldn't form right.

She turned her back to him, still holding one of his arms, which she pulled over her shoulder. "Other hand." He held it up, and she grabbed it, pulling him onto her back. "Wrap your arms."

He could barely fumble them around her neck, but with her help, he managed it. Then she picked up his legs under her arms and carried him on her back down the tunnel. Slowly. So slowly.

They didn't make it far. Artie was just too scrawny and small to carry Putnam. She fell to her knees, and he slid to the ground.

She barely paused—which even in his state of grogginess Putnam found admirable—but moved into a better plan. Taking off her inner cloak, she ripped one seam so that it turned almost back into the blanket it had originally been. She slid it under Putnam, who lay down on his side again, and then she began to pull the blanket like a sled behind her, dragging Putnam down the tunnel with her.

The floor of the tunnel was quite, quite comfortable under his blanket as he slid along. This was a fine way to die, thought Putnam. Of all the possibilities, it could be much worse. He could barely even feel his back anymore. It still burned, but behind everything else. He could ignore it and sleep.

"Don't fall asleep," barked Artie.

But as they slid along, around curves and corners and along the endless tunnel, Putnam began to drift off.

Then Artie snapped him awake again. "What is *that*?" She stopped pulling, and Putnam's sled stalled. "*That.* Putnam, *look.*"

Putnam didn't even open his eyes. He was facing the wrong way to see whatever it was she was looking at anyway. "Hallucination," he said dreamily.

Suddenly she was yanking the sled faster than ever, running with the sled sailing behind her. Putnam was flying. Into the hallucination, whatever it was, with Artie. He sighed and slept.

3

ARTIE AND PUTNAM.

*W*HEN ARTIE was at her most exhausted and low, pulling a sled with her possibly dying friend in it to nothing and nowhere in a dark tunnel underground, that was when it happened. Around a curve: more light.

Lots more light.

So much it was hard to see.

She squinted into it. It wasn't just brightness. There were things *in* the light. Plants? She could hear . . . birds? Running water? Was she imagining?

If so, it was the best fantasy ever, and she wasn't planning to stand outside in the cold. She could feel drafts of warm air wafting up the tunnel from the bright place.

Putnam said it was a hallucination, but she didn't think so. Or if it was, it was a dream they could share, so why not go to it? She ran into the light, yanking him behind her. She almost flew. She ran as much out of fear for her injured friend as joy for the light.

Then the tunnel opened out and she was in—was it a giant cave? Made of sunlight? And was she standing on *dirt*?

The slick tunnel floor ended in leaves and grass and mulchy composty soil that smelled of plants and decaying things and worms and life. Above her, light glowed, but she could not see the sun or the blue sky. It was brighter here, underground, than it was outside, as if this strange place trapped and reflected and lengthened the available light. Everything was green and growing, warm and humid and alive. A squirrel-like creature ran past, chattering. Brightly colored birds flew overhead. The grass and bushes and trees rustled as if to say *welcome* and *safe*.

Artie couldn't help it. She fell to her knees. She felt like she was praying, except she didn't know who to thank. The bears? Herself and Putnam? God, whoever he or she might be? The cave itself, pulsing with life as it was?

Finally she said, "Putnam. Putnam. We're here." Wherever *here* was didn't matter right now. She could tell immediately that this was a place without bears.

But Putnam didn't answer, and when she turned back to him, her stomach fell. They were safe and warm, but he was terribly injured. In the light she could see that his face was slack in unconsciousness, bloody and swollen. But far worse was his back, dark with blood—some drying, some still wet—seeping through the cloak she'd tied around him.

She patted his face. He felt warmer now. Carefully she pulled the sled blanket over the mulch and into a patch of sunlight, where she pillowed his head under a folded-up section of blanket. Then she stood and looked around. What could she use to help stop bleeding?

For herself, back on Tathenn, she'd always used moss for wounds. Clean water to wash, and moss to dry and pack under a bandage. After one more glance at Putnam's sleeping face, she followed the sound of water and found two streams coming together: one cloudy, the other clear as crystal. The merged stream, cloudy like the smaller stream, tumbled away happily.

She tasted the joined stream: it was unpleasantly salty, brackish just like the ocean. She sipped from both of the little streams above where they merged.

The cloudy stream was so salty she spat it back out, gagging. The clear stream, however, was pure and fresh.

So: water, both for washing wounds and for drinking.

And though the banks of one stream were salt-covered and dead, the banks of the other stream were covered with moss, enough to pack many wounds.

She ran back to Putnam and slowly dragged the blanket to the river. Putnam bumped over every little hill and rock in the grass, but it couldn't be helped. She knew she was long past the point where she could carry him. Exhaustion seeped into every bone in her body.

Sheer willpower kept her moving. After positioning Putnam as close to the stream as possible and opening his clothing in back, she took the empty water sack and filled it, pouring as much salt water as possible onto the wounds. It would sting, but the salt water would clean the cuts.

He barely even groaned, which she knew was a bad sign. When she used to clean her own wounds with salt water, they'd stung severely, especially the deep cuts. Putnam didn't even open his eyes, didn't flinch.

She could see the cuts clearly now. Claw marks. Huge. Five long ditches, from his shoulder to his lower back, deep enough to put her pinky into all the way to the end of the nail, had she wanted to. He was lucky none of the claw marks were on his spine—they bit into tender flesh, but that was it. No bone showing.

When she'd gotten the cuts clean—and they'd turned pink and bloody all over again—she packed them with moss, ripped his ruined cloaks into bandages, and tied them around him. Neither of them needed a cape in this warmth, and they were left with two blankets (her old cloaks, still bloody) to use for other things. She laid the bloody capes in the clear stream, weighted with stones, to wash clean.

Hours after they arrived at the sunny underworld, Putnam was asleep on his side on the now-dry sled blanket, surrounded by rustling grass, as clean and cared for as possible. In addition to moss and fresh water, Artie had found some unfamiliar berries growing on a bush, and she'd tasted one—just one—and spat it out, feeling fine. An hour later, she ate one berry; it was delicious, and she still was okay. Later today she'd try a handful, and if that went well, she'd give some to Putnam when he woke. As she scouted the area, she also found carrots growing wild, their lacy tops inviting her to pull and find the food beneath, and mint running rampant as always wherever it landed, and finally a bush of cloudberries, which she ate by the handful, her stomach growling. She picked some for Putnam and placed them in a little pile on a flat stone about the size of a plate, on the corner of the blanket. Then she returned to the clear stream with the carrots and the lone water sack.

On her way back to Putnam, full water container and freshly-washed vegetables in hand, she detoured to the tunnel they'd emerged from. How did the ice keep from melting?

She placed her hand on it, expecting it to be cold and slippery with melt. Instead, it felt smooth and slick like a well-polished rock, and warm to the touch.

It wasn't ice.

She scratched with her fingernail, then rubbed her fingers over the slightly oily surface so familiar to everyone on her island. It was gypsum, a rock easy to find there (especially in the north) and almost magical in its many colors and properties. Soft enough to be carved, strong enough to use for making statues and other objects. Sometimes translucent enough to use for windows.

They'd started their journey in snow and ice; she knew that. She remembered the bitter cold. But somewhere in the deep of the tunnel everything around them had transformed. She remembered not feeling cold as the trek went on—even feeling warm as she'd pulled Putnam's limp body the last part of the trip. She'd shed each layer of clothing to protect him, and each time the cave had warmed enough that she'd not died of cold. She hadn't thought at the time what a gift that was.

Of course, the cave hadn't transformed *because* she took off her cloak. It just felt that way.

On each side of the tunnel, the gypsum walls of the cave veered off into underbrush and tall grass and, above her, toward the sky—or what *looked* like sky, white and hazy. Shouldn't it be night? But light glinted off the walls. She couldn't see where the gypsum walls stopped going up and curved over to become ceiling. She looked out at the land. The trees were sparse—more like a garden gone wild than a forest—but the hilly ground made it impossible to see far.

Her exploring didn't bring her to any of the other walls

of the cave—though she was convinced this place must be just that: a giant cavern that somehow glowed. And how did the light work? Did the gypsum somehow trap and enlarge it? Because it was so much brighter in this cave than it would be out on the surface.

This world made no sense. The bears and their island, too. Or maybe the deep south made sense in its own way, and that was different from how the rest of the world worked. Maybe it had a different logic.

Finally, with the carrots and water, she returned to Putnam, who was still sleeping. His face looked so calm, even full of bruises. She smiled. She'd been full of bruises when they met, and now it seemed to be his turn. He'd taken her in, and now she'd take care of him.

Exhausted, she curled up next to him and fell asleep, the warm sunlight on her face.

WHEN PUTNAM woke, he turned onto his back before he realized what a terrible idea that was. Gasping with pain, he rolled to his side, and then, slowly, hitched himself up to sitting.

Several things occurred to him at almost the same time: first, his back was burning, and second, his face hurt to move. But his back: he'd never felt such pain. It felt like fire had been poured over his shoulders and run down.

Next he noticed where he was: on the blanket, but no longer

in the ice tunnel. Artie lay near him, asleep and curled into a little ball on her side, facing away from him as if guarding. The world around them was green and fresh, full of birdsong and squirrel chatter and bubbling brook and scented with mint and lilac and other flowers he couldn't name.

Then he thought: *I'm so thirsty. And hungry.* And as he thought these things, he saw the filled water bag and the carrots and the berries, so he ate and drank, saving some for Artie.

By the time he nibbled his last carrot, everything had come back to his waking memory: the trip to the deep south; the bitter winter; the ice; the bears, the bears, the bears. Artie dragging him into the tunnel. The long tunnel. His deciding to sleep and to die.

Was he dead? Was this the afterlife?

He took another bite. If so, carrots in the afterlife were good. Very good. But wouldn't the pain be gone if he were dead?

Artie rolled onto her back and stretched her arms and legs out, basking in the warm air—so foreign to them for so long. Then, in a flash, her face became watchful and her body pulled itself in. Her eyes popped open, glaring for a moment before she focused on Putnam—and smiled. "Hey. You're alive."

"I wondered," said Putnam. "You're sure we're not dead?"

"I'm sure," said Artie. "I dragged you in here myself. It's the end of the world, but it's not anything worse."

"How?" He meant *how does this world work?* And *where are we exactly?* And a bunch of other things, too. But for once the words didn't come to him. He gestured around him, and Artie nodded as if she understood.

"I went back to the tunnel while you were sleeping. It's not ice anymore. It's gypsum. You know what that is?"

He nodded, trying to understand.

"We're way underground, someplace warm. The good part is that there's food here, and we won't freeze, and there don't seem to be any dangerous animals."

She meant the bears. It was a relief to be safe from them.

"The bad part is . . . we might be stuck here."

He nodded again. The thought had occurred to him just before she said it. There was no way they could get back up the steep slide they'd come down. "Well," he said, thinking out loud. "We won't believe we're stuck until we've explored the whole place carefully. Unless you already did that?" He wondered how long he'd been sleeping.

She shook her head quickly. "I was too tired. I just washed you off, and found food and water, and went back to the tunnel to look—"

"You did a ton!"

They sat in silence for a moment. Putnam realized Artie was probably thinking along the same lines he was. What if they *were* stuck in this cave forever?

"There are worse places to be stuck," he said. "Anyway, this is what you wanted, right? To get far away from Tathenn?"

But that didn't seem to make her happy. "I didn't take us here on purpose!" she said. "I wouldn't have done that to you. I wasn't trying to get us stuck." Her hands balled into fists.

"I didn't think you were!" Putnam leaned toward her, groaning a little as his back adjusted. "You saved me, remember?"

"And you saved me."

Putnam grinned and winced at the same time. "Let's not keep bringing this up over and over again."

Artie scooted behind him and gently pulled up his shirt and peeked at the wounds. "I can get more moss for packing. And maybe we should wash the wounds again."

"I think I remember that part a little," said Putnam. "It really hurt. The water burned."

"Salt water's good for wounds." Artie's gentle hands paused on his back. "That's what *you* wanted," she said, as if she were thinking something through. "You wanted to find the source of the salty sea."

She was quiet so long that Putnam wondered what her point was or if he'd missed part of the conversation somehow. "I did want that," he said. "*Do* want it. And I'm sorry my exploring brought us here—I didn't mean for that . . ." He felt terrible. This was all his fault.

"No, that's not what I mean," said Artie. "Not at all. I was thinking of the water. There are two streams. One is fresh."

"And the other one is salt?"

"The saltiest water you ever tasted. That's what I bathed your wounds in last night."

"So you think . . ."

"The source of the salt. I think we're close to it. Maybe if we follow that stream, we'll find it." Still behind him, she gripped his shoulders, and Putnam could hear the excitement in her voice. "Even if we can't get out, you can still do what you came to do. You can still save our world. You can stop the ocean from turning to salt."

"*We* can," said Putnam.

4

PUTNAM AND ARTIE.

*P*UTNAM WANTED to explore. His back and shoulders did
not want to explore. His back wanted to die, it wanted
to throw itself in a snowbank and freeze, it wanted an end to the
constant burning and the sharp pain every time he moved. But he
himself—his brain and heart—wanted to find the source of the salt,
be the hero, make the world's water drinkable again. And he would
do this even if his back were twice as clawed up as it was now.

At least, he thought he would. He certainly wasn't going to
find another bear and test that idea.

He couldn't see the claw marks himself, but Artie had as-
sured him they were "impressive-looking." Parallel tracks running from his right shoulder all the way down his back.

He took a deep breath and felt the wounds stretch slightly. He
and Artie were walking along the salty creek, having left behind
the place where the sweet water forked into it. There was no path,

but the land was all grasses and bushes and scattered trees, and except for the constant hills, it wasn't too difficult to navigate.

Around them the grasses rustled. There wasn't a breeze in this place, exactly, but there was something more than a draft. Air was moving. And this morning, after the light dimmed for a couple of hours and then returned, he'd waked to a light rain, almost more of a drizzle.

Artie interrupted his thoughts. "Ahead. Look."

They rounded a hill, and the sound of water suddenly increased to a dull roar. A waterfall.

A waterfall, and next to it a tall willow tree. And something else. A statue.

A statue of a woman.

THEY STUDIED the tree and the waterfall and especially the statue. The waterfall, as tall as a tree and maybe twice as far across as Putnam could have jumped, caused a fine mist to linger in the air, leaving everything in the area wet and verdant. Artie scrambled up the rocks on the side of the cascade and stood on top, reporting that as far as she could tell, the river that fed the waterfall wound its way out of some nearby hills.

The tree curved over the stream, casting restful shade all around the wide, pond-like area where the water foamed from its crash down the waterfall and before it began burbling away down the stream. The willow draped itself over the water almost like a woman pulling a bucket from the river for cooking, one limb trailing into the stream.

Artie returned from her climb and together they studied the statue, which stood straight and tall in the spray from the waterfall, dripping. It was the figure of a girl, maybe a couple of years older than Putnam and Artie. She wore a simple old-fashioned dress, no shoes, no cold-weather gear. Arms at her sides, hands open. Something about the posture seemed wrong, as if she'd been told to pose. Uncomfortable. Putnam thought she looked angry, and then he thought sad, and then he thought—he wasn't sure. All the mist condensing and dripping down her face made her expression impossible to read.

As he studied the statue, he realized the problem wasn't just that the statue was standing stiffly, but that, with the water running down it in constant rivulets, it had an odd feeling of movement to it. The overall impression was troubling; it unsettled him.

He turned and walked away, but Artie called him back. "Did you notice . . . ?"

"Notice what?" He looked at Artie, not the sculpture.

"She looks . . . she looks like Raftworld. Like your people, I mean. Like Raftworlders."

He forced himself to look again at the girl. The waterfall misted her head, and water dripped down her cheeks in tracks. Artie was right. She did have a classic look about her—not Islander, with their straighter hair and sharper features, but Raftworlder, with tightly-curled hair, here pulled into braids, and a warmer (he thought) face. Well, maybe not warmer; maybe just a face he was more used to. Artie's face certainly seemed warmer now than he'd originally thought.

"She does look Raftworlder, right?" Artie said. "The braids?"

Putnam nodded. "Old-fashioned hair and clothes for Raftworld. But yeah. I can see it." He turned away again, wanting to get out of here, away from the misty water, away from the weird statue.

"Isn't that weird, though?" Artie said exactly the word he was thinking, but it sounded like she meant something different by it. "I mean, doesn't it make you wonder? How she got here? Who carved her? And look—how is she even standing up?"

"What do you mean?"

"There's no base. For the sculpture. She's just standing on the wet ground. How is she even staying up? How is she not falling over or sliding into the river?"

The figure stood precariously close to the water, on the very edge of the stream. Sand shifted around her feet, and water swirled at her toes, but she did not shift.

Not she, *it*. Just a statue.

"It is strange to find a statue where there's no people," he said, cautiously agreeing. "I mean, I guess that proves that someone, maybe someone from Raftworld, arrived here a long time ago . . ."

"And carved a statue?" Artie sounded almost accusing. "Why?"

"I don't know. I'm tired." And it was true. Putnam suddenly felt exhausted, like he couldn't think clearly, and like he could barely take another step. And he just didn't want to talk about the statue right now. "I need to . . . find somewhere to sit."

Artie, who'd been crouching to examine the woman's feet, jumped up. "Oh, I'm sorry. I should have thought. You need to rest. Let's find a place to settle for a while."

"Away from the water," said Putnam, shivering. The mist suddenly felt cold.

Artie ran off and reappeared a moment later. "Just up here." She led him uphill, away from the waterfall and the tree and the sculpture, to a warm sun-dappled spot in a meadow under some tall bushes, where she spread a cape-blanket and said, "Sleep. I'll find some more food, and I'll come back soon."

He nodded, so tired he couldn't argue, couldn't suggest that he'd look for food, too. Could only sleep in the sunshine.

WHILE PUTNAM slept, Artie went exploring. First she found more berries and carrots, and then she found some small tomatoes and something that looked like oversize apples. She carefully picked two; she'd try them in small bites before letting Putnam eat any.

She also found an aloe plant and broke off a couple of the fat, gel-filled leaves. When Putnam woke, she could help his back heal. Aloe worked wonders; she'd used it herself many times.

When she went back to Putnam, he was still sleeping. She tied the food into a blanket corner and left. Just for a short time. Not for long.

She returned to the statue.

There was something that drew her back, and she wasn't sure what it was. The expression on the girl's face? The fact that she seemed like a Raftworlder? That she looked only a couple of years older than Artie herself? The hopeless set of her shoulders?

The statue was in the same place as they left it. Of course it was. It was dripping with mist and spray from the waterfall. Artie stood in front of it, her heels in the shallow water of the stream, and looked it in the face. She was shorter than the statue, but not by a whole lot. The stone girl stared downstream. The water blurred her features, made her look sad. Maybe that was what was bothering Artie: all the mist made it look like the girl was crying.

Artie reached up with her sleeve—damp by now from the waterfall mist, too, but she found a dry spot on the inside of her forearm—and carefully wiped the statue's face. There. That was better. The face looked so much more peaceful without the water dripping down it.

Except.

Except it was still dripping.

The light mist hung in the air—barely a breath of water; it would have to build up for some time to form rivulets down the statue's face. And yet the statue was crying.

The statue was *crying.*

Tears were coming out of her eyes. What Artie had thought was mist on her face wasn't mist at all—or rather, it wasn't *just* mist.

Artie watched closely as the tears ran down the girl's face. Then down her neck and chest and torso and leg. The tears ran off her foot and into the water. The tears ran into the stream . . . that eventually fed into the ocean.

Tears!

A wild thought in her head, Artie stepped back into the water. She walked a couple of yards downstream of the statue, dipped her hands into the water, and scooped a gulp into her mouth. Spat it out again. Salt. Salt as strong as could be.

She walked back to the statue and then upstream several yards, where she repeated the experiment. She drank. And drank again.

The water was clean and pure. Upriver from the statue, it was sweet, the way water should be.

ARTIE THOUGHT about running back to Putnam to tell him that she'd located the source of the salt. But what could they do to fix it? What would Putnam want to do? Chop down the statue? Destroy it?

No, they couldn't destroy the statue. It—*she*—was crying. Artie didn't know what the right thing would be to do, but she knew that killing the statue wasn't it.

Because, yes, it felt like they would be killing someone. Artie didn't know why. No, she did: there were stories on her own island of people who'd been cursed and turned to statues. Fairy tales, she'd always thought. But now, with this weeping statue in front of her, she thought there might be some truth to the stories.

Maybe, just maybe, this statue was once a real person.

If Artie could just get the statue away from the water, then she could keep it from infecting the ocean with more salt while she considered what to do next. She pushed as hard as she could, her shoulder set against the stone, but she couldn't move the rock. The statue wasn't fixed to a base, but it was locked in place somehow. She couldn't even jiggle it.

Exhausted and sore from pushing, Artie flopped down on a big stone that lay partly in the downstream water and rested her head on her elbows. It seemed almost like the statue was looking directly at her face.

It was still crying.

"Why?" Artie said.

She knew the statue wouldn't answer. She wasn't stupid. But somehow it felt—like maybe the statue would listen. Like there could be a one-sided conversation that might actually go somewhere.

"We found you," she said, trying to be conversational, "almost by accident. I mean, my friend was looking for you. But he didn't *know* he was looking for you. He wants to fix the salty sea. To change it back to fresh water. That's why he's on this trip in the first place."

The statue's tears continued to fall. She was expressionless. Studying her, Artie could see how asymmetrical her face and body were. She'd probably never been thought a beauty. Misshapen head. Turned-in feet. And on her arm, a set of claw marks similar to Putnam's.

Had she also faced a bear, before she found this cavern? Had the tunnel saved her as well?

"Maybe you ran away like I did. That's how you ended up here." The statue couldn't hear her, not really—and definitely couldn't respond. Artie rolled her sleeve to show the old burn marks on her arms and brushed her hair back to show her face. With her new bruises from the tunnel, she was surely ugly enough to impress this statue. "I don't have claw marks like you and Putnam. But—I do, kind of." She'd had her own bear, in a way.

The world vibrated with the not-quite-silence of stream and waterfall and birdsong. Artie looked around. This underworld was good. Maybe this girl had once lived here in peace, long ago. And now Artie was here, safe from all kinds of monsters.

"I'll figure something out," she said, half to herself and half to the statue. "I won't let Putnam destroy you."

The statue almost seemed to sway. But no, it was Artie, sliding face-first down the wet rock. She stopped herself by plunging her hands into the water and hopping up. It was time to go anyway. Putnam might be awake.

"I'll be back as soon as I can," she said. It felt nice to talk to the statue. Like she understood. Artie turned and waved before heading back to Putnam.

5

PUTNAM AND ARTIE.

*P*UTNAM WOKE in the afternoon, his back burning again. He realized that when he'd walked around earlier in the day, thinking his back felt like fire, he hadn't yet known what fire felt like. *Now* it felt like fire. By comparison, before had been like the discomfort of a bad sunburn. He was reminded of his father's cook, who had gone into labor early one morning, before she'd expected to, and the doctor had arrived and asked her how bad the pain was, compared to how she'd felt before labor, and she'd said, *I've never had a baby before—I've never done worse than sprain my toe. How can I compare stubbing my toe to having a baby? It's bad!* But of course, it got worse before the baby was born. He, Putnam, had never been clawed by a giant bear before; how could he know what it would feel like or when it would be at its worst?

Still, he hoped this was the worst.

Artie's hand brushed his forehead, and he opened his eyes to see her worried face above him in the sunlight and greenery. They were shaded by a large bush, on a blanket in the grass. He was on his side, and his bottom arm tingled like it had fallen asleep. Nothing, though, compared to his back.

"Feverish," Artie murmured. Her worried expression deepened. Putnam closed his eyes and fell asleep again.

He woke briefly in the almost-dark, Artie curled up on the blanket near him, sleeping. The gypsum walls barely glowed.

When he woke again, it was morning, and the blanket was damp with dew or rain. Artie had rolled him to his stomach and had removed the moss from his wounds—the breeze playing across his back, excruciating, snapped him awake. He groaned.

"This will feel good when I'm done. I hope," Artie said. And then something cool hit the burning stripes on his back, and her fingers were gently smoothing it in.

"Ice?" he said. He couldn't think what else it could be. But it didn't feel like ice. It felt soft.

"Aloe. I found some nearby. Tried it on myself first to make sure it was really aloe." She paused to squeeze some more of the gel onto his back, and he almost cried with relief.

He fell asleep again, her hands lightly moving on his back. She was singing, quietly, something about mangoes.

The next time he woke up, he was lying on his other side,

his back once again packed with moss. Underneath the moss he could feel the aloe at work, though, and his back wasn't burning quite as sharply as before.

"Artie?" He lifted his head carefully. It must be afternoon by now—though it was hard to tell time in this bright place. Artie wasn't around—probably had gone to look for food again or something. With the amount he was sleeping, she'd be done exploring this entire underworld by the time he recovered.

In front of him on the blanket lay some more berries and the water sack and a few mint leaves. He propped himself up long enough to eat and drink, finishing with the mint leaves, which made his cottony mouth feel much fresher. He lay down again, chewing the leaves and feeling better than he'd felt since the bears had attacked.

He tried not to think about how they were stuck here.

And how he hadn't fixed anything.

ARTIE REMEMBERED nursing her mom in the final days of her pneumonia—trying to get her to eat, cleaning her up, changing dirty linen, washing her face with cool cloths. How none of it worked. And afterward, when her mother was gone, there was no protection for Artie, no one who cared about what happened to her. No one who loved her.

But this wasn't then. She kept telling herself that. Putnam

would get better—was *already* getting better. She'd left him after putting another layer of aloe on his wounds and covering them with moss and turning him on his side. She'd laid out food and water in case he woke. And she'd tiptoed off for a little time by herself.

All her old memories were coming back to her here, partly because Putnam's sickness made her remember her mom and partly because the statue's clawed arm made her feel her own burned arm more sharply—and partly because she had so much free time and quiet, which bad memories always seemed to want to invade. She'd hoped to escape from everything in her old life, to live away from Tathenn, and to be safe. And instead she was here with someone sick, someone she cared about and didn't want to lose, and all of a sudden she felt unsafe again. Like the deep memories she'd buried away—the really bad ones—were going to return to her. Like she might get burned all over again. Might burn up until there was nothing of herself left.

Pretty soon she was sitting on the river stone in front of the statue. She didn't even know how she'd gotten there. And she wanted to talk. She wasn't sure why.

She'd left Putnam sound asleep—but he wouldn't come here even if he woke. There was no danger of him overhearing anything she said. And the statue couldn't repeat anything. This would be the perfect place to say things that she couldn't otherwise say.

The statue would listen. Or if not listen, it would sit there and cry with her. The statue wouldn't be surprised by anything Artie said, wouldn't tell her that things that were done to her were her fault, wouldn't say she should have stood up for herself better, wouldn't suggest she should have left sooner than she did, certainly would not say she should move on and put everything behind her. Though tears would drip down her stone face and into the stream, the statue wouldn't say anything.

What a dumb idea. How could just talking help anything?

The light was waning, slowly moving toward night. She stood on the damp stone. Her clothes, wet with mist, felt clammy and cold and heavy in the half-light.

The statue glimmered and—it looked like it moved.

A hallucination or a trick of the light.

But maybe not a trick. Maybe the statue really moved. A tiny bit?

Its head was tilted in a small bow, as if to say good evening.

"Um. Hi," said Artie, staring. She felt like the girl could hear her—which was silly—and she wasn't sure what the proper etiquette was. "I have to take care of my friend. But I wonder if maybe—maybe we can talk sometime?"

In the shadows it looked like the statue nodded again, just a fraction.

Artie bowed, in the formal old-style way of Raftworlders, a style that she'd only heard about in stories. She turned and went to Putnam.

PUTNAM WOKE from a dream in which the statue was trying to tell him something but he didn't want to listen. She was . . . she was telling him to *stop*. He lay with his eyes closed, trying to remember the wisps of dream before they were gone forever. He had . . . he had an ax in his hand, and she was yelling, *Stop*. Was he going to chop her down?

He yawned. His back felt much better. It still hurt if anything happened to touch it, and the skin felt tight. Every time he moved, he could feel the wounds on his back stretching and aching. But if he didn't move, he felt pretty good.

He sat up, slowly, a little dizzy with the exertion of it. He couldn't see Artie, but he could hear her light, humming voice drawing nearer. She was figuring out a tune; he could tell from the way that she kept going over the same runs again and again. Like an exercise, but much nicer to listen to.

Then he could see her coming up the trail—for there *was* a trail now, a thin ribbon of matted grass that she'd walked back and forth on, probably leading to the river.

Sure enough, she carried the water sack. "I thought you might want more."

He nodded his thanks and drank. "The food was good, too."

"Are you better?" She picked up the remaining aloe leaf, but he waved her away. That could wait.

"Yes, I'm much better. Thanks to you." He was hungry,

actually. But that could wait, too. "Where've you been? I mean, besides the river? Anything interesting?" He mostly wanted to know two things: Was there a way out? And what was the statue doing there?

"Oh." She looked shifty. "Mostly I've just been to the river. And to pick berries—they're on the other side of the hill. And I found a little apple tree with giant apples." She picked up the sole apple on the blanket and held it out to him. "Go ahead. I already ate one. They're not poisonous or anything."

He almost laughed at the idea of checking apples for poison, but she seemed serious. Grateful for the food, he took it and bit in. The fruit was sweet, and as he ate, juice dribbled down his chin. He felt suddenly ravenous, and though the berries and carrots had been good, they weren't enough to fill his stomach. He wasn't sure the apple would be enough, either.

She watched him as he ate, a look on her face that he couldn't read. He wondered if she'd been to the statue again. Of course she had—it was right next to the river. It still bothered him, gnawing at the edge of his brain. "Did you get a chance to study the sculpture?"

Slowly, she nodded. There was something she wasn't saying. He could tell.

There was something Putnam wasn't going to say either. In his dream, the statue had looked like him—like a slightly older, girl version of him, or maybe his dad when his dad was a teenager. Like his sister—if he'd had one. She looked so familiar. It was eerie.

"She definitely looks like—well, like Raftworld," said Artie, as if she'd read his mind. Or maybe she was thinking along the same lines. "She's been by the river a long time, I think."

"I don't like her," said Putnam. "She's creepy." He couldn't shake the feeling that there was something very wrong with the statue. Maybe he was supposed to destroy it. Maybe that was what the dream was telling him. "Can we move that thing? Knock it down?"

"Why would we do that?" Artie asked quickly. "She doesn't move, anyway." She looked for a second like she was going to say something more, but she didn't. "I'll get you some food."

She left and came back a few minutes later with more apples. As he ate, Putnam realized what else bothered him about the statue. It was the pulling feeling that had led him all the way here—the feeling that he *had* to come south, and that once he came south, he'd know what to do—the feeling that had deserted him when he'd felt the intense pain of the bear's claws.

Seeing the statue had brought that feeling back. He felt the thread again in his gut, pulling him toward—toward *her*.

6

ARTIE AND PUTNAM.

*A*RTIE DIDN'T tell Putnam about the statue's crying or about how the water was sweet above the statue and salty downriver. He already wanted to knock the statue down; what would he do if he knew its secret?

Artie wasn't stupid. She could read what it all meant. The statue's tears were running down the river to the sea, turning the ocean to salt. The tears must be magical, saltier than normal tears, to do that much damage to an ocean—even if the statue had been crying for many years. The sleeve Artie had used to wipe the statue's face had dried, coated in a thick white chalk of salt. Her shoulder—pressed against the statue to push—had also turned white. Only after drying in the sun for several hours had the thick salt patches flaked off like dried mud.

So why didn't she just tell Putnam? After he ate, she rubbed more aloe on his wounds. Each of the five angry gutters on his back glowed red and scabby, but none looked infected anymore. As she eased the gel into each long ditch, she considered how easily Putnam could destroy the statue. It was only made of gypsum, so far as Artie could tell, and wouldn't be hard to break. Gypsum was a soft rock.

Artie couldn't let him. There was, she was sure, a person in there. Artie had seen her move. Hadn't she?

But Putnam had been sent on a mission . . .

She cleared her throat, hands still on his back. "What if . . . what if you never find the thing that is making the sea turn salty? I mean, what if you don't fulfill your mission? Will your dad and everyone—will they be mad?" She didn't add, *And will the ocean become unlivable?*

He finished his apple and set the core down on the blanket. Cleared his throat. "I . . . have something to tell you." He sounded serious.

Artie, finished with his back, wiped her hands on her leggings and moved to sit in front of him. "What?"

"I didn't . . . I didn't exactly get sent on a mission."

"What do you mean? You aren't trying to find out why the water is salty?"

"No, I'm trying to figure it out," he said. "And fix it. But I wasn't *told* to. No one sent me. I just sent myself." He picked up the core and tossed it into the bushes, then winced and groaned.

Artie peeked at his back. He hadn't broken any of the scabs open. "Maybe don't throw for a while."

Putnam nodded.

"So. Basically you just ran away from home?"

He nodded once, jaw set.

"Are you—are you planning to ever go back to Raftworld?"

His eyes flipped up to stare at her. "Of course. I only ran away until I could figure out the salt and fix it. Fix the ocean. Then I go back."

And he'd return a hero. She could see the pull of that, how exciting it would be. That is, if people love you and admire you already, then saving the world would make everything even better, because you'd be proving to them that they weren't wrong to care about you.

"What if you don't figure it out? Then what happens when you come home?"

He shrugged in a closed-off way that reminded her of herself. "I never thought about that."

They both sat for a moment. Artie wasn't sure what Putnam was thinking now, but she was imagining if she returned home after this journey. It was hard to even predict how angry her stepfather would be and how he'd take it out on her. She couldn't think what Putnam would be facing. Why go back at all?

"Well," she said in what she hoped was a cheerful voice, "if we're lucky, we'll never find out, because you won't have to go back. Because we don't have any way to get back to our boat anyhow."

He stared at her for a moment, then broke out laughing. Like she'd said something really funny. He laughed so hard his eyes filled with tears.

PUTNAM REALIZED Artie might think he was laughing at her, so he explained. "It's the idea that I don't need to worry about getting into trouble. I just think that's funny. I mean, I'd much rather be able to get home, even if I'm in a little trouble."

"I don't get why that's funny," Artie said.

"I guess it's really not."

Artie said, "We're kind of in the same boat. Both runaways." She smiled.

In the same boat. Putnam hadn't been given a mission of any kind; he'd just run away. He wasn't any better than her. Worse, really, since it seemed like she had much better reasons for running away than he did, at least according to all the bruises he remembered, and the old scars she carried.

And although he'd finally told her the truth, he hadn't told her the *whole* truth: the fight with his dad, his shame over how his dad ruled—not being willing to take action, just letting things happen. His anger over how his dad let his second mom leave. And now, his guilt over running away himself and how much, even though he was mad at his dad, he missed him. Artie never talked about her stepdad, and he could tell she didn't miss him. Her life had been so hard. Putnam was ashamed of how easy his life had been—and how he still couldn't handle it. Artie's stepdad had given her the bruises, Putnam was sure of it. His dad had only given him—what? Hard words? He felt like an idiot for getting upset about that.

He was happy, though, at how much better Artie looked now, even with the new bruises from the ice tunnel: healthier, stronger, more filled out, and calmer. Not all the time; she was terrified of the bears, much more than he was. When they'd faced the beasts, she'd frozen in fear. But even so, she'd helped him escape, too. And here in the underworld she seemed genuinely happy. She still didn't sleep well—up and down all night long, and always surprised when she woke and saw him, as if she'd forgotten that he was there and was scared of him.

But her smile was readier and more real.

"Stop staring."

"Sorry," he said. "I was just thinking—this is kind of perfect for you. I know you didn't plan it, but you said once that you wanted to live somewhere where there weren't any people. And here we are."

She blinked. "I'll help you find a way back."

Putnam grinned. "Did you change your mind? You want to go home?"

"Not home." Her voice was low and sounded almost angry. "No. But if I went back with you, maybe I could find a little island to live on, back in the warm part of the world, and you could go home. *You* want to go home, right?"

"Of course." But he was beginning to see that there was no *of course* to that question, not for everyone. "There's an island Raftworld sometimes visits—it's small with a deep lake in the middle. There's good food, especially mangoes—and tiny monkeys for company. You could live there, probably. And I could visit you when Raftworld stops by for mangoes."

Artie nodded. "I'd like that. To see you."

"Okay, then. I'll get us out, somehow. And we'll find the boat—or build a new one—and we'll get home."

She looked like she wanted to believe him, very much.

He didn't tell her that before they left he was going to study that statue. As weird as it seemed, he felt like the statue was what he was looking for, the key to the salty water. Maybe if he destroyed it . . .

But he didn't tell that part to Artie. She probably wouldn't understand.

She had a secret, too; he could tell, something she wasn't telling him about the statue or about the underground cavern. Like she knew something he didn't. Part of him wanted to know what it was, and the other part of him wanted to pretend that everything was okay, that they'd find their way out of here together and go back home, where they'd both be fine.

DAYS PASSED as Putnam healed and Artie explored and found food. And the days in this underground world lasted so long! Artie couldn't get over it. The first night they were there she had noticed the difference in light from the surface. The gypsum walls seemed to soak up light during the short southern day and then glow with it for hours after the sun must have set. By the time the glow faded fully, it was almost day again. Full darkness lasted only a few minutes.

And it rained every morning. All Artie could figure out was that, high above, the ceiling of the cave must have condensation on it from the humid air that warmed up and dripped down when the sun rose. Or maybe it was so high up that there were actually clouds; she didn't know. Once Artie and Putnam learned to pack up their blanket before the rain fell, they were fine. They let themselves get showered, and they dried off once the rain ended.

Every morning she visited the statue and studied it, but it didn't move again. She talked to it. She said, "Please stop crying" and "How do I make you stop crying?" and "I need you to stop turning the sea to salt or Putnam might knock you down," but nothing worked. She pushed from different angles every day, but the statue didn't move. She even kicked it a few times, and nothing happened except her toes hurt.

Truthfully, it was hard to worry about the statue every moment. This garden was flawless. It felt to Artie exactly like she and Putnam were swaddled into a little pocket of the world, protected and hidden away. Like they were hidden inside some giant being's luck pouch. It was impossible to imagine this world with bears—or anything scary. This lucky pocket of an underworld simply couldn't hold terrifying things like that. Only lovely things. Only good reminders. And once Putnam's back healed, everything would be perfect.

She did think of the statue sometimes. And the claw marks on her arm. And then she put them out of her mind, deliberately, like she was hauling out trash to the bonfire and then walking away from her old home. This place was safe. It had to be.

She hated the thought of going back to the outer world. This little pocket world, this was for her. She'd crawled inside and she never had to come out. She could almost feel a god's heart through the fabric of this world, beating.

She'd said she'd leave because she knew Putnam wanted to go back to Raftworld. *Needed* to go back. His father must miss him. And Artie knew, too, that if her mother were alive, Artie would try to get back to her; she could understand Putnam's wish to return. So she'd help him find a way out, and then she'd break it to him that she was going to stay here. Where it was safe.

But even as she thought about staying, her heart said, *What about Putnam? Won't he miss you? And won't you miss him?*

Finally, early one morning, she plunked herself down in front of the statue and just sat, wondering again how such a thing had come to exist. Putnam was still asleep. Several days had passed, and every day made him stronger. His back was healing. The scars would always be there, ugly and deep—she wasn't a doctor, after all, and couldn't do anything to make them fade and not pucker—but he would live. His arms and legs and everything worked well, and the tightness in his skin and back muscles seemed to lessen each day.

Meanwhile, she had a good hour or more until Putnam woke and the rain came. She sat quietly on the big rock, and this time she didn't tell the statue to stop crying. She just talked.

"Hey," she said, stretching her toes into the water. "I'm sorry you're sad. And I'm sorry your arm got clawed up. I bet it was a bear, like Putnam's scar. I'm glad you got away from it. My arm . . ." She paused, thinking. She'd never said what happened out loud. "It wasn't a bear. It was my stepdad. He was really mad, about a whole bunch of things, and he threw the pan of hot oil, and it got all over my arm and my neck. He threw it at me." She wasn't telling the story right, but the statute didn't seem to mind. "That was all after . . . after my mom died."

She kept talking. For a long time.

The statue never frowned, never judged; she just listened.

WHEN SHE reached the end of her story, she stopped talking. It wasn't really the end. There was more to talk about—good memories of her mom as well as the sad and bad memories—and she could tell the statue these stories, too. But for now, she'd said enough. And she felt—lighter. Unburdened.

"Um," she said. The statue *almost* seemed to lean forward slightly. "I've been hogging all the talking. I just realized that. Do you—do you want to tell me anything?"

For a moment there was complete stillness in the garden, except for the stream quietly babbling. The birds fell silent; the crickets and cicadas ceased their chirping and humming, the bees stopped buzzing, and the leaves did not rustle—as if waiting for something important. Except for the stream, it felt like time itself had stopped.

Then the statue bent its head, just a fraction of an angle. Maybe a trick of the light.

And then it blinked.

Blinked again.

And then it opened its mouth and began to talk.

7

PUTNAM AND RAYEL AND ARTIE.

*P*UTNAM ROSE early—a sure sign that he was feeling better. He woke just as Artie was leaving, but he lay still anyway and let her depart. She was up to something. He wanted to know what it was.

She headed toward the river, and after a few moments, he pushed himself up to sitting to follow her.

It was harder than he'd thought it would be. Up until now, he'd really only left the blanket to take care of necessary business at a nearby latrine Artie had dug for him. This walk, though, was much longer and took him back through bushes and long grass. He wondered how Artie had helped him up the hill into the sunny spot to begin with; he barely remembered the walk and the river; even the icy tunnel had faded into a long dream of pain and claws and burning.

But he remembered the statue. Or he thought he did. Did

she really look like a Raftworlder? How was that possible? He must have dreamed that part.

Trying to be quiet, he walked slowly and stayed on the path. The grass was flattened, as if Artie took it often. Well, of course she did: to gather water for him. But the path was so worn it almost looked older than their arrival here. Or she was using it much more than he'd thought.

He could tell he was nearing the river because the sound of the waterfall grew loud. He could see the tall willow tree bending gracefully at the base of the fall; the statue would be nearby. He paused on the path. Was Artie down there now? How would she feel about him barging in on her?

All at once the entire woods went silent; it was as if his ears suddenly stopped working—except that he could hear the water running and splashing. And through the babbling water came the sound of a voice.

Not Artie's voice.

A Raftworlder accent, but old-fashioned, the way the oldest of the elders spoke. "My name is Rayel," said a girl's voice. "I want to tell you a story."

As PUTNAM listened, the statue told her tale of how she left home to avoid an unwanted marriage; how she found her gift for the cold; how she met and lost Nunu; how she found

Una in the underworld; how she and Una fought; how Una left. How Rayel, the girl who couldn't freeze, felt herself hardening in grief and regret, how she turned into a statue, how she cried.

She didn't cry as she told her tale, though.

Putnam, creeping closer, could see Rayel through the brush. Her face moved stiffly, as if unused to speaking, and her voice was creaky with disuse. Her hair was curled as tight and dark as Putnam's, twisted around her head in intricate braids.

"What about the scars on your arms?" asked Artie. Putnam, who didn't remember, smiled. After all that—the crazy story, the fact that a statue was talking *at all*—Artie wanted to know about scars on the statue's arm. She was an odd one.

"The bears," Rayel said. "Like what happened to you two. Bears follow everyone who comes south. Everyone has a bear after them."

Oh. Putnam gasped, then remembered he needed to be quiet.

Artie too sounded shocked. "But the bears didn't—they didn't kill you."

"I was already a statue when they found me. Mostly."

There was a long, long pause. Then Artie said, in a small voice, "Wait. Your bear came *here*? Into this underground world?"

"Yes."

"But . . . I thought this place was safe."

"Safe as anywhere else. Which is to say, not safe. Eventually your bear will find a way in, just like mine did so many years ago."

Putnam sat back with a crunch of twigs. The bears could be here—anytime. He thought of all the nights he'd slept without fear, out in the open on the grass. Artie, too.

Artie turned and saw him, and he could see the same thought in her face.

RAYEL HAD been frozen so long. It was as if the cold had finally, in her grief and shame, found her and had frozen her all at once. She didn't know how the magic worked. She just knew that, when it happened, she had embraced it. She'd *wanted* to freeze. She had never planned to thaw.

It hadn't occurred to her that her tears would affect the rest of the world. She'd never considered that.

If she had considered it, would it have made a difference? She wasn't sure.

But when Artie started speaking, she had felt something inside her come to life. Here was someone else with a story just as painful as hers—maybe more so; pain was so hard to compare and weigh. It was always heavier in your own hands than in anyone else's. At any rate, here was this other girl with a painful story. Rayel listened, and her heart cracked open.

Then the magical words: *Do you want to tell me anything?* And Rayel found that she did. Most of it confession. All the anger she'd felt toward Una (and Nunu) for leaving had melted away over the years, and what was left was regret and shame over the way she'd treated her. Thought of her. Rayel also felt grief, pure and sharp like a sword in her heart, for the people she'd loved and lost: Solomon, and Una and Nunu. And now, she felt love for Artie, who had gone through so much and still had room in her heart to care for someone else. And she worried that Artie would get stuck, too, and freeze. Underneath all these feelings, she was angry that the world was still, after all these years, so hard on people.

So many emotions. They stirred her. She could feel waves of energy tingle all the way to her fingers and toes. And she knew she was unfrozen now for good.

Everyone she'd ever known was dead—too many years had passed. But here she was, brought back through this girl's story, and through her own. The least she could do, given that she'd been unfrozen, was help this girl in return.

And the boy, Putnam. He'd listened to Rayel's story, too. She knew that—she'd heard him and seen him eavesdropping early on, and she'd decided to keep talking, for him as well as for Artie. He was, according to Artie, a Raftworlder, and Artie cared about him. Rayel wanted him to know her story.

As she told her own tale, her body thawed. Her limbs began to move. She felt stiff, as after a too-long sleep, but she was alive. Living and breathing again. With someone who cared about her—and people she cared about. Sharing a story with them. A perfect moment.

When she finished, Artie asked if they were safe here in

the underground. Rayel told the truth—*no*—and Putnam fell backward into the bushes, and the perfect moment was over.

THE THREE of them moved to the side of the willow tree that was farthest from the waterfall, so that they were more out of the mist, and Putnam and Artie sat with Rayel for hours, rehashing her story and fitting it with their own histories. It turned out that Putnam was a distant grand-nephew of Rayel's— through the baby that hadn't been born yet when Rayel left. And he *had* heard stories about Rayel—not her name, which was probably recorded somewhere but not in the tales he'd heard, but her actions: he'd heard about a king's daughter who'd run away on her wedding night and never returned. He'd heard— though he didn't tell Rayel this part—that the princess had been cursed and turned into some kind of monster and had left. In some versions she left in order to protect her people from herself, and in others she was chased out after killing the young prince in a fit of rage and jealousy. She'd gone somewhere far, far away where she could be a monster in peace.

Maybe, Putnam thought, lots of monster stories were just that—stories about people who'd left, for whatever reason, long ago. Maybe a hundred years from now, he and Artie would be remembered, if at all, as monsters who'd been exiled to the deep south . . .

"Una never came back?" asked Artie. "Nunu?"

Rayel shook her head. Her hair and skin looked less stone-like, and she moved more freely. "Not that I know of. I think—I think something must have happened to her. I think she *would* have come back."

Putnam said, "How did Una get out of here?" That part of the story didn't make sense to him.

"Weren't you listening?" said Artie. "She swam—"

"I think he means how could she swim up to the ocean from here. And even if she could swim that far, how could she survive when she got to the freezing ocean above?"

Putnam nodded. That was exactly what he'd meant.

Rayel shrugged. "This stream must travel underground before it empties out into the ocean." She paused, as if waiting for them to say the rest.

"Maybe she transformed as she swam," said Artie. "Into Nunu."

"There are Raftworld stories about dolphin people," said Putnam. "But I didn't know they were *real*." Bears, dolphins; he wondered how many fairytales were telling the truth.

"I like to think she turned back," said Rayel, "into whatever she really was, and she got away, and had a good life somewhere warm." She leaned her head back against the tree. "But I guess I'll never know." Her face was full of color now, and her hair shone with the light glancing on it. Her clothes, old-fashioned but beautifully woven, moved like real fabric now, in bright colors. She stretched and then said, "Well. I guess you two need to get back home. I wonder . . ."

"Do you want to come with us?" asked Artie.

"I was hoping you'd invite me," Rayel said, dipping her head awkwardly.

Putnam said, "Of course! Please come. In fact," he said, trying to smile, "you're actually next in line for the throne—"

"Don't be silly," she said. "I *never* wanted that. Just . . . don't make me marry someone awful." She grinned.

Putnam laughed. "I'm pretty sure you'll make your own choices. I mean, technically, you're really, really old."

And then it struck him: all this talk of going back, and he still hadn't fixed the water . . .

Oh.

It was her. "The salt in the ocean. Your tears."

Rayel nodded.

So. The problem he'd come south to fix was already solved—and not because of anything he'd done. It felt a little disappointing. Shouldn't there be more? A big finish of some kind? A fight against a dragon, maybe—or *at least* a giant sled made of salt that had to be hoisted back into the sky?

"We fixed it," said Artie, leaning back on her elbows and then sliding down to lie on her back. Her eyes were shining. "Well, Rayel did, anyway."

"After causing the problem in the first place," Rayel murmured dryly. "And it will take a while for the ocean to heal. It won't be suddenly better just because I stopped crying."

Artie, curled up on the grass, giggled.

She *giggled*. Had she ever done that before, during all the long weeks of their trip?

So many things had happened since they arrived at the cavern, and all he'd done was lie around with a sore back. He'd return to Raftworld—if they even *could*—exactly as he was, not having *done* anything. All his problems still the same.

"What's wrong?" said Rayel softly. "Artie told me her story. But I haven't heard yours. Want to talk about it?"

He shrugged. "There's really nothing to tell. I'm the king's son. My life is practically perfect."

"I was the king's daughter, and my life wasn't perfect."

She waited.

"I had a big fight with my dad before I left," said Putnam. It was hard to admit that. His dad wasn't perfect, but he was a good dad, especially compared to some.

"Does he love you?" asked Rayel.

Putnam looked at her, startled. He almost said, *Of course,* but stopped himself. There was no *of course,* not for everyone. "Yes. He does."

"And you love him."

"Yes."

"Then when you go back, you can fix it. You can."

Artie was fast asleep, her head pillowed on a tree root.

Rayel said, "And your mother?"

Putnam took a deep breath. "She left us. Left me. She didn't—she didn't love me. Not enough to stay, not enough to come back." It was the hardest thing he'd ever said. And he knew that this was the thing, more than anything else, that made him angry with his dad. Why didn't his dad go after her? Why didn't he make her stay? It was the thing behind every argument he and his dad had. It was the thing that made Putnam—the next king, the kid who had everything—feel small and unloved. And there was no way to fix it.

Rayel put her hand on Putnam's. It was warm and pulsed with life. "I'm so sorry," she said.

AFTER A FEW MINUTES, Rayel nodded toward Artie, who was still asleep. "She's exhausted. Caring for you, and visiting me. She figured it all out a long time before you did, you know. And she did the only thing that could make me stop crying. She told me her story, and she listened to mine. Just listened."

"What exactly happened to her?" asked Putnam. "What did she tell you?"

Rayel stared at him, her black eyes piercing.

"She hasn't told *me* anything," said Putnam. He almost

added, *It isn't fair.* And it wasn't, was it? He'd helped her sail the boat here, given her his food, saved her from bears almost at the cost of his own life, traveled with her for so long and never been anything but nice to her. He should get to hear her story, too. What had hurt her so badly?

"I don't think you understand how this all works," said Rayel. "I told my story to her and to you—and yes, I knew you were in the bushes all the time—because I wanted to. Because I wanted you both to know.

"But Artie hasn't given you her story. She told *me*, because I was a statue and that was all she could bring herself to talk to. She didn't tell you. And the fact that you were nice to her doesn't mean you get to hear her story. It's *hers*, don't you see? She doesn't have to tell you. She doesn't owe you anything."

"But that's—"

"Not fair? People don't owe you their sad stories just because you're a good person, Putnam." Rayel looked over at Artie, and a softness flashed across her face. "She gave you her friendship. That was a lot. A lot."

He nodded. It was, and he knew that. He also knew that her friendship was different, *better* than any he'd had before (his mind flashed to Olu and his schoolmates). And it was brave. From Artie, friendship took so much of what had already been stolen from her: trust and openness.

"It is a lot," he said. "She's the best friend I've ever had."

Rayel tilted her head to the side.

"I mean, she's friends with me without caring that I'm going to be king of Raftworld someday. Without caring that I'm a really good sailor and raft builder, and that I can read and write really well. Without thinking that I'm tall or good-looking or that I live in the nicest house on Raftworld. She's just my friend because of . . ."

"Because of you," said Rayel. "And because you are in this mess together."

Putnam said, "We can't stay here." It was a question as much as a statement.

Rayel nodded.

"But we don't have a way out."

"We could use the tunnel Una and I used when we went to the surface to explore." And Rayel told him about the tunnel with the gradual incline. "I think it's probably still there," she said slowly, tapping her head in thought. "It was really wide. It's probably how my bear got in."

Putnam swallowed. "The bears. Do you think—"

"They'll find you? Yes, eventually. Mine found me." She held out her arm with its claw marks still embedded in it, even though her arm was now flesh. The cuts were deep, like farrows that had been dug for planting and then abandoned.

"*Mine found me?*" repeated Putnam. "What did you mean when you said everyone has a bear after them? Your bear wasn't the same bears that are chasing us?"

"Of course not," said Rayel. "That was a long time ago." She paused to think. "Like I said, we each have our own bear. At least, that's my belief. And I had a long time to think about it, after I took care of mine."

Took care of? "What did you do?" asked Putnam.

She smiled, but the smile didn't look happy. "I don't recommend my method."

He waited.

"I ate it."

"*What?*"

"I can't explain it, exactly. I was already a statue, or mostly one anyway, and the bear found me. It clawed my arm. The worst pain I'd ever experienced. And I was so mad—about everything—I just grabbed it, grabbed it and hugged it to me, and it—it shrank, and when it was small enough, I put it in my mouth and I ate it. I was so angry. I thought my anger could . . . devour the bear."

"Did it—did it work?"

She shook her head. "It's been clawing my insides ever since. Until Artie and I talked, until she told me her story and I listened, and then I told her mine."

"And now the bear is gone?"

Rayel shook her head. "Now it's a little more quiet. Napping, maybe. I really don't recommend eating your bear."

But what do I do? Putnam knew he couldn't fight the bears. Not again. Not ever. He'd lost last time; he'd lose again. And now he knew what it felt like to lose, how much it burned. He'd fail even faster next time around.

One of those two bears was his, and one was Artie's.

"Your bear never leaves you," said Rayel. "That's what I've finally learned. Your bear follows you. If you run, it will chase you forever. You can't run away."

Artie opened her eyes, which glittered in her shadowed face. She looked empty. Putnam wondered how long she'd been awake. "So if the bear never leaves . . . then we need to find another way. Not fighting it. Not running away. Something else." She spoke in a slow, sleepy voice. Maybe she was still partly asleep. She turned on her side and her eyes closed again, her face restful. "I like this tree." Her hand curled around the root that pillowed her head.

Putnam said, "I'll get our stuff—our blankets and things—and bring them here, and we'll all stay together tonight. And maybe tomorrow you can show us the way to get out. And you'll come with us."

Rayel smiled. "That sounds good." She lay back next to Artie. By the time Putnam returned with their supplies, both girls were deeply asleep.

THE NEXT morning, the three of them packed up, though there wasn't much to pack. Artie and Putnam tried to share warm clothes with Rayel, who reminded them that she didn't need them. She'd told them yesterday, but in the mix of everything else—a statue come to life, bears tracking them—they'd forgotten that she didn't feel the cold.

Artie and Putnam needed to make their clothes as warm as possible. They had thought that Putnam's two cloaks and his shirt were ruined by the bear, but now, cleaned and dried (though still torn), the cloaks still had some warmth to give. So Artie and Putnam each wore one of the ripped-up capes as their underlayer and kept a mostly whole one to wear as an outer cape. Even the outer cloaks, however, were torn where Artie had made them back into blankets and used them as bandages. There just wasn't much *cloak* left to any of the cloaks. They'd need to get to the boat quickly—and hope it was still there.

They still hadn't talked about what to do about the bears. Artie was hoping they wouldn't meet up with them. Rayel had said the bears wouldn't stop looking; she hadn't said the bears would *find* them.

They ate as much as they could for breakfast (several apples, carrots, handfuls of berries) and they packed up some apples and carrots in an extra hood, along with some potatoes Artie had found and dug up that morning. They put on their boots and found their mittens. And then all three of them started walking in the direction of the tunnel Rayel had used, so many years ago.

Rayel didn't talk. She'd started coughing that morning, first just a few coughs and now more and more, racking her body and making her hold her stomach. Putnam had asked if she was sick, but she shook her head and insisted that they leave right away. She'd be fine.

As they walked, pausing frequently to allow Rayel to cough, Artie divided her thoughts between worrying about Rayel—who *did* seem sick—and thinking about the bears. Artie had heard most of the conversation the day before. She'd been dozing, but the mention of bears had brought her out of that dreamland and back into reality with a crash. This world wasn't safe. The monsters were coming. And even Rayel, who'd been here so long, didn't know how to defeat them.

". . . Artie?"

With a jerk, she realized Putnam had been talking. They'd reached the edge of the garden, and there in front of them was a tunnel into the gypsum, wide and smooth, gradually ascending. Big enough for a bear to get into or out of easily.

Rayel and Putnam were both staring at her, and she realized she was breathing short, upset breaths, almost like she'd been running.

"Sorry," said Artie. "Daydreaming."

Rayel coughed again, doubling over and clutching her gut.

"Let's rest here for a few minutes before we go up," said Putnam.

THEY HAD a snack, and Putnam thought maybe everyone was feeling better. Rayel didn't eat, but she had stopped coughing. Artie had eaten a lot and seemed less upset. Putnam raised his arm to toss his apple core and grinned when it barely hurt to throw. Of course, if he had to lift anything heavier than an apple . . . He winced.

"Are you okay? We can rest longer." Now Artie looked worried about *him*.

"I'm completely fine," said Putnam, trying to sound as confident as he must have sounded before they'd been attacked by the bears. Trying to *feel* that confident again.

"Okay, then." Artie stood and brushed herself off, then held out her hand to pull Putnam to standing. He didn't need it, but he grabbed her hand anyway. Rayel gave him his walking stick—a long straight branch she'd found near the willow tree. The stick helped when his back got tired.

Suddenly Rayel's head jerked back, and so did Artie's. They'd heard something.

And a second later, Putnam heard it, too. *Growling? And from where?*

Putnam shook his head, and the sound was gone. "What was that?"

"Maybe nothing?" Artie said. She sounded like she wanted to believe herself.

Rayel stifled a cough and nodded, lips pressed shut in a line.

They stood a moment. They'd all heard something—a breeze, a birdcall, something—and maybe just imagined it as more? Or maybe it *was* more? And was it coming from behind them or in front of them? In the echoes of the tunnel, Putnam couldn't tell.

Either way, there was only one exit from the underground world.

They headed up the tunnel.

8

PUTNAM AND ARTIE.

*T*HE TUNNEL was wide and followed a long, gradual slope, much nicer for hiking than the one they'd come down. The ice was rough, which made it easier to walk on without falling. Putnam tried to imagine Artie dragging him down this tunnel on a sled made of blanket, and shook his head. They were lucky they'd come down the other passageway. It had been narrow enough to allow them to escape, and slippery enough for Artie to pull him on the blanket.

This one was so wide, a bear could navigate it.

Walking behind Artie and Rayel, Putnam was almost sure he could hear something padding slowly and carefully behind them (or maybe in front of them?) and stopping just a split second after they stopped for each rest break. But he didn't know what to say or do. Maybe, just maybe, what he heard was a trick of sound in the cave, the way your own steps echo in tunnels *just* after you've finished walking. Then Rayel would cough, and the sound would seem to stop for a few minutes. Maybe he was imagining.

He didn't ask Rayel or Artie about the noise again. What if the answer was that they heard it, too? The tunnel was their only way out.

They walked a long time, rarely speaking and only then in quiet, clipped sentences. Somehow going back to the surface made everything seem dangerous again. The tunnel grew darker and darker—and then, slowly, it grew brighter and brighter until finally a light glowed ahead of them. Putnam put out his bare hand to feel the walls. Pure ice now. Their breath exhaling in steam. He was glad of the cloak—and knew it would be even colder outside.

Rayel coughed quietly, like she was trying to muffle the sound.

"Ready?" breathed Artie.

"Ready," said Putnam. "Let's go."

The three of them stood side by side—the cave so wide now that they could do this easily—and walked the last stretch until they reached the tunnel's opening.

They stood near the top of a slight hill, somewhere near the boat. Putnam thought he recognized the land. It was a clear day, and they could see the water from where they stood. "That hill," said Artie, pointing. "That's the one we climbed before. I'm almost sure of it. The boat should be on the other side."

Rayel nodded. "That's about where my boat was, too."

Even if it wasn't the right hill, it was high, and they'd see more from there. And thankfully it was not too far away. Putnam nodded to Artie, not trusting his voice, and they started walking. Putnam's back was aching from the long hike already, and he leaned heavily on his staff.

But they had taken no more than a few dozen steps when all of them heard a sound. A *definite* something, directly behind them.

A low, rumbly sound, like a growl.

Rayel fell to her knees, coughing and hacking.

Artie and Putnam turned at the same time—and there they were. Two bears. The same two bears, it seemed like. Rising up from the snow. Either the bears had been underground, and had just now followed them out, or they'd been sitting outside in the snow as the three had left the tunnel and walked past them.

The bears blocked their escape back to the tunnel—not that that would have helped anyway. And there was no way the three of them could beat the bears to the sea, even if Putnam weren't injured and Rayel weren't now on her knees, coughing and choking. Even if they were sure of the boat's location—and if their boat was even still there.

Putnam gave up. He'd already stood up to the bears once—and almost died. *Would* have died if not for Artie. He knew what the claws felt like. He could not live through them again. He stood in the snow and felt every ounce of bravery leave him.

ARTIE SAW THE BEARS and heard Rayel cough and felt Putnam freeze next to her, and she felt . . . angry. She knew what claws felt like—she'd felt them most of her life. But she did not give up. Not this time. Not ever again. Her usual tactic was to wait things out—or to run away. But she was done with waiting. Done with running. Done with it all. Just *done*. It was the one word that formed and hardened in her head at this moment. *Done*.

She put her arm out to tell Putnam and Rayel to stay back. She had this.

And she faced the bears.

She didn't plan to die. It wasn't a suicide mission. She just thought, *Done*.

Also, she didn't plan to wait for the bears to attack.

She attacked them.

For a millisecond, just before she ran at them, she wondered what the bears were thinking. Usually—at least in stories—bears were hungry, they wanted food, they were on the hunt. But these, she knew, were more than bears. They wanted more. They did not give up. They did not tire, and they never would.

To Artie the bears looked like everything she'd run away from, always coming after her, never leaving her alone. Rayel was right. *Your bear follows you,* she thought. *You can't run. You can only take care of it.*

And knowing all that, she ran at the bears. She aimed for the one without the bloody forehead. That one was Putnam's; somehow she knew. Hers was clear-faced. She flew at it across the ice and snow and leapt into its arms. A great bear hug, her arms around its neck, its mouth gaping open in surprise.

PUTNAM FROZE. What was Artie doing? Putnam's bear—the one with the mark on its forehead—stood still, as confused as Putnam. Both watched as Artie hugged, then choked, the bear.

Artie's bear began to shrink.

Right before Putnam's eyes, her bear grew smaller. Soon Artie and the bear were the same size, and a moment later, she was hugging something the size of a large dog as it wriggled and twisted and tried to get away. Then she was kneeling and the bear was the size of a puppy. Her back was to him, but she called over her shoulder, "Putnam, you too!"

Rayel was on her hands and knees in the snow, heaving like she was throwing up. The bears ignored her.

Artie yelled again. "Putnam!"

He looked at his own bear, who was mesmerized by what was happening to his companion. Now, if ever, was the time to attack. He gulped.

Putnam could still feel the claws in his back. How could he run at this thing? But Rayel kept choking and coughing, and Artie screamed, "NOW!" and he knew he had to. He ran at his bear from the side, swung his staff around the bear's head, and leapt on its back, gripping the staff with both hands and hanging from the bear like a cape, the walking stick the clasp around its neck.

The bear bucked, but Putnam held on like death, bringing his heels in to grip as well. He could hear Artie yelling but couldn't hear what she was saying. Maybe Rayel was yelling too. He couldn't tell.

After what seemed like an eternity, his own bear began to shrink. Then his feet touched the ground, and he was standing over it, holding it down. Then he was bent over it, still gripping. As his staff fell to the ground, he clutched the bear with his hands; it was the size of a puppy and then even smaller.

Rayel coughed one last racking cough, her hands cupped over her mouth. And then, finally, silence.

"Are you okay?" Artie said, and Putnam started over to Rayel, dragging his toy-size bear along, but the older girl lowered her clasped hands and gasped, "Finish with your bears. I'm fine."

Putnam and Artie each held their own bear. Both creatures were tiny, about the size now of baby birds, small enough to hold in one's cupped hand. The bears clawed and growled and bit, but all they were able to do was leave little raised scratch marks on Putnam's and Artie's exposed wrists and snap at their fingers, which through the mittens felt ticklish. Putnam's bear yanked off one of his mittens and couldn't seem to figure out how to spit it out. He shook it in his jaws like it was an animal he'd conquered.

The bears were, in fact, almost adorable now, thought Putnam, if you could overlook the fact that they still wanted to kill you. They were tiny and pathetic predators, but they didn't seem to know it, so they kept scrabbling. Artie grabbed hers by the scruff of its neck and dangled it out from her body, where it kicked its legs and growled so weakly it sounded almost like purring. Putnam copied her, first tapping his bear on its nose to make it drop his mitten onto the snow.

The two friends stood for a moment, studying the miniature killers. Then Putnam set his on the ground behind him, expecting it to . . . run away, maybe? He wasn't sure. It didn't run away; it scurried up the back of his legs instead and bit at his neck, little nips that stung like ant bites. He pulled it off and held it out again.

Artie observed him silently.

Rayel sat in the snow, hands clasped tightly in front of her.

"What do we do with these things now?" Putnam asked. "It doesn't seem like they're going to stop following us."

Artie shrugged, studying hers intently.

"Why are they so small all of a sudden? They're almost cute—"

"They're *not* cute."

"No," he replied quickly to her sharp tone. Then he added, looking at his bear more closely, "No, they're not cute at all." His bear still had a blood mark on its forehead from where he'd fought with it before. It had been so busy hunting him it hadn't taken the time to groom itself. Or maybe that was a permanent stain.

Artie stared into her bear's eyes. It was flailing its legs to escape her grip, but not succeeding. In fact, it almost looked like it was still shrinking.

"What are you doing?" he asked.

"Don't eat it," said Rayel. Her voice was raw from coughing.

Artie didn't answer except to grunt with effort, still glaring into her bear's eyes. The little bear hung its head, now shrinking so quickly that it was almost snapping away to nothing. Putnam gaped—he could feel his mouth dropping and his own bear nipping at him and wriggling, but he didn't care. He watched as Artie's bear dwindled until it was the size of a stone. Something you might toss in the water to see it skip.

Artie flipped her hand over to hold the bear in her palm, and suddenly it quivered and froze—like water turning to ice but much faster. And in her hand was a perfectly shaped terrifying bear made of ice. Putnam reached out and touched it with his bare finger. No, it was made of gypsum. Artie opened the luck pouch that hung around her neck and dropped it in, an unreadable expression on her face.

Rayel breathed, "*Yes,*" and bent her head over her cupped hands.

Putnam turned to his bear, not sure what to do. Artie didn't have magic any more than he did, so how had she done it?

At his shoulder, she whispered, "Look it in the eyes. Tell it that you know what it is. Tell it that it won't chase you anymore, because you won't run away. Tell it that you'll live with it and carry it around, but it doesn't scare you anymore. It doesn't own you. It can't kill you."

The words didn't make sense, exactly. *I know what it is?* But Putnam did it anyway. He looked into his bear's eyes, and thought, *I know what you are.*

And suddenly he did know. The bear was everything he'd lost, all the sorrows he'd ever faced and ever would. And he knew then that he'd carry the pain of his mother leaving for the rest of his life, and maybe he'd never really be able to explain it to anyone, and Artie would carry her own wounds, and so would Rayel. They'd never completely get rid of them, they'd never get over the bad things that had happened. They would carry these things around; they would never put them down because they weren't put-downable. But that wasn't the point. The point was that the bad memories wouldn't freeze them, wouldn't kill them.

As he thought all these things, his bear shrank to almost nothing and quivered to stone, just as Artie's had. In his hand was a terrifying little figurine, all sharp edges and teeth and claws. "It'll cut me."

"Sure," she said. "Don't carry it in your hand. When we get back to the boat, I'll make you a luck pouch. And you can put it in there."

"But it's bad luck," he said.

"That's okay." She sounded tired. "The pouch is for things that make you *you*. Bad as well as good. It's just that I—it's just that most people only want to carry the good."

She held out her hand for it, and he handed it to her carefully, so as not to cut her. She slipped it into her luck pouch. Then she turned to Rayel. "Want me to carry yours, too? Until you have somewhere to put it?"

And Putnam saw with surprise that Rayel was holding a small stone bear, too. She handed it to Artie. "I'm glad to get that out of me."

THEY WALKED up the big hill, and there was the boat, still floating in the current like a miracle. Artie sighed, relieved to be able to go . . . well, home. To go home, wherever that might end up being.

Putnam had been quiet since Artie put the creatures in her luck pouch. Now he said, "What's it feel like?"

Artie knew exactly what he meant. "It's the first thing in my luck pouch. Well, the first three things—but you'll both get yours back on the boat." She didn't say what it felt like, though.

Putnam would find that out for himself, and she was pretty sure Rayel already knew. It felt like a sadness was lodged there, pressing lightly on her chest, and some pain and terror, too, and it would be there always. But there was also a power to it. She had something she'd lived through. She felt strong.

And she knew it was only the first item. There would be more things to put in her luck pouch, eventually.

"Now let's get on that boat," she said. "And go home."

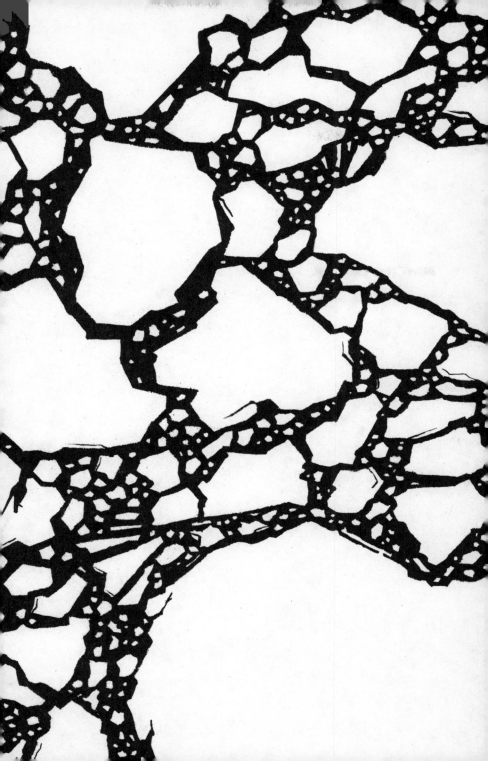

PART FOUR

Return of the Lost

All Three. The Present, and a Little Bit of Future.

ONCE UPON two times, two girls and a boy and a magical dolphin-girl and their bears all went on journeys. They arrived at various destinations, but the destinations weren't always as expected. Bad things happened and good—and sometimes both at the same time. Most of the travelers transformed, some of them drastically. No one knows where the dolphin-girl ended up. Some stories don't have happy endings, and other endings are mysteries.

But one story—*our* story—needs a finish. Two girls and one boy returned to the warm part of the world, in a little miraculous boat, sailing slowly outside the current, through the quiet and sweetening sea, heading north, always north. Eventually they arrived.

They sailed to Putnam's world, to Raftworld. It was also Rayel's world, though it was the wrong time. Still, the more they talked it over, the more she thought she would stay there. Or maybe, eventually, she'd move to the Islands or travel somewhere she could experience winter and get to use her gift. But for now at least, she'd visit Raftworld. She had a lot to catch up on.

Artie thought she'd stay on Raftworld, too, at least for a

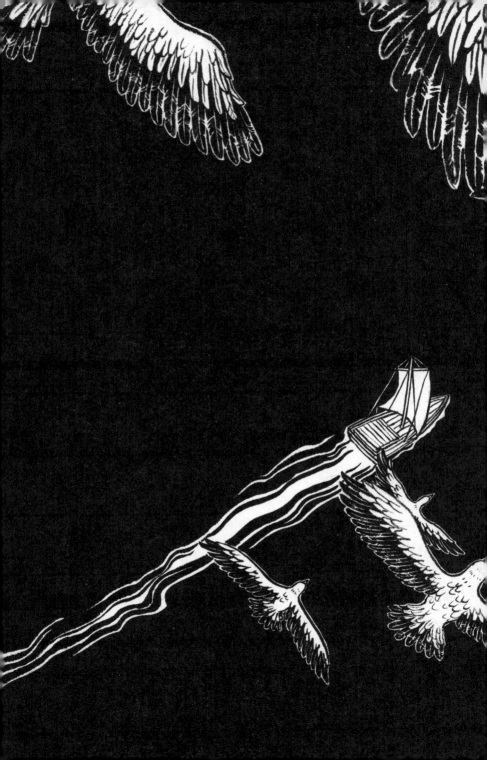

while, with her new friends—especially Putnam, this person almost as close to her now as her own heart. This person who'd saved her—and whom she'd saved. Later, Artie thought, she might move to the small secluded island with the monkeys and mangoes, and live by herself. But that idea sounded less and less right as time went on, and besides, for now she owed it to Putnam to go with him and face his father and whatever punishment he might receive.

Putnam hoped Artie would change her mind and stay on Raftworld, though he knew he couldn't make that happen. But he wished. Maybe, he thought, if he'd had a brother or sister, he would already have known what it was like to have someone that you're willing to die for and are also completely irritated by—at the same time. Someone who you know so well that you know what they're thinking, sometimes, before they even open their mouth. Someone whose face is almost more familiar to you than your own. He thought that might be what a sibling was like. He'd never had a friend like Artie, someone who would never, ever flatter him or lose a game to him on purpose or hide her mood from him. Who would always be true.

In their little boat, they spotted Artie's home island late one afternoon and sailed around it without landing. They stayed far out to sea, keeping it on the horizon. Rayel stared, hungry for people after so long. Artie watched, arms crossed, as they circled and moved north.

Just north of the big Island, they saw what Putnam had hardly dared to hope for: a shadow on the horizon. Raftworld. He let out his breath in a gush. How would he have found Raftworld if his father hadn't waited for him? If the nation hadn't lingered, hoping the king's son would return?

The three travelers arrived to Raftworld in the early night, a couple of hours after dark. The half-moon gave enough light to see but not so much that they would be noticed. They were all glad; they could step into this world without crowds. For Rayel and Artie, there would be explaining to do, some of it hard to believe. For Putnam, there would be apologies to make and groveling to do; he couldn't imagine his father not being furious at how long he'd been gone: well over a month, going on two.

They all hoped to tell their stories in private.

They pulled the boat up to the south dock—the quietest dock at night and closest by a little bit to Putnam's house—and walked down the empty path to the king's mansion. Voices wafted from people's homes, muffled. The water slapped lightly against the bottoms of the rafts, which shifted as they walked.

Artie, who had never been on Raftworld—nor on any boat bigger than the fishing boat they'd traveled the seas in—marveled at the size of Raftworld. Rayel, who had been there before, marveled at how familiar it seemed, even with a century of changes. Hundreds of small rafts, joined with waterproof seams that allowed for flexible movement on the water; a house on each raft, surrounded by a lush, dense garden; the nighttime sounds of chickens nesting and children protesting bedtime. Paths wound through the rafts to draw everyone to the center, which was magnificent: huge gardens spanning multiple rafts; a large building that served as school, market, and meeting place; and the king's mansion, not much bigger than the other houses but set in a gem of a garden that, even at this time of night, glowed with small lights.

At the entryway to the king's garden, Putnam paused as if uncertain.

Rayel said, "Is this the place?" It was bigger than she remembered.

"Are you scared?" Artie said to Putnam. She thought, *Of course he is.* She'd be scared, too. What would his father do to him, after he'd been gone so long without permission?

Putnam took a deep breath. "It'll be okay. He'll be mad, but he'll also be happy to see me. To know I'm safe. He'll be glad that we—that Rayel—fixed the water. And of course, he'll love to meet you both. I just—I'm thinking about how much he must have missed me and worried."

Artie took one hand and Rayel took the other, and they stepped through the gateway and into the garden, through the garden and into the house, through the house and into Putnam's father's arms.

The old man wept with joy.

RAYEL, ARTIE, and Putnam felt funny about being called heroes. They hadn't slain monsters, defeated bad guys, conquered foes. They had shrunk a few bears, but that victory was private. And they'd stopped the salt from entering the ocean—but only after Rayel had started it in the first place. Still, the people called them explorers. As Raftworld traveled north, the water grew less salty by the day, almost by the hour. And someday, all the ocean would be sweet again.

Rayel moved into a small house near one of the hydraulic engines; she said she wanted to learn how they worked, as she might plan another exploring trip into the cold sometime—maybe the deep north this time. She promised not to leave without telling anyone. And she made new friends—starting with the Raftworld storyteller, who was excited to meet someone who knew so many old legends.

Artie was given her own bedroom in the king's house, a small cozy room next to Putnam's. Putnam attached a lock to the door, in case she wanted to lock it. She did.

Artie's bedroom contained a soft bed, and clean clothes to change into, and a cozy chair next to a window where she could sit and watch birds flutter and plants grow.

She went to school with Putnam, where she learned reading and knitting and how to build small rafts and how the giant hydraulics worked on the corners of Raftworld. Sometimes, to help out, she mended nets. She got a lot of compliments on how well she mended: the patches she sewed, full of intricate stitches like a spider's web, turned out stronger than the areas that had never torn.

One day, Putnam's father took Artie to a house where there was a woman musician with a double-stringed instrument made from gourds. The instrument was shockingly hard to play, so Artie went to the woman's house every day to learn.

Weeks passed. Weeks and weeks. And they were all good. She still had nightmares, but the days were sunny and sleep was bearable.

One afternoon as they sat on the south dock, back-to-back in the sun, eating strawberries out of the same bowl, Putnam asked Artie if she still wanted to go to the little island and live by herself. "No one will bother you there if my father tells them not to. I promise." His back was stiff against hers, but his voice was calm and careful. He was making the choice all hers.

Artie ate the last strawberry, licked the juice off her fingers, and put her hand to her luck pouch. The little stone bear shifted under her hand's weight and then stilled—moving so slightly that it might have been her imagination. In addition to the stone bear, her luck pouch now held a fragment of the first string she'd broken learning to play the kora; and the tiny pencil stub she'd first learned to write her name with. And there could be more things later, more reminders of goodness and bravery and, yes, of pain and trauma, too. This world was so many things, but one of them was that it was sometimes good. The pain would never go, and maybe not the fear either, but there would be brightness as well. And people to love. And a whole life to live.

Artie reached back and squeezed Putnam's hand. He squeezed in return, still waiting for her to speak.

"I want to stay here. With you."

They held hands, slightly sticky from the strawberries. With her other hand, Artie lightly traced the dotted scars on her neck and running down her arm. She was made of constellations. And she alone could decide what their shapes meant, because these stars were all part of her. Dragons and goddesses and dolphins and whatever else she decided. She had survived so much, and so had Rayel and Putnam. Whatever happened next, they weren't alone.

"Let's find Rayel," she said, "and see if she'll tell us a story."

AUTHOR'S NOTE

FANTASY STORIES are about escape. We read them to disappear into a new world, someplace where our own complicated problems can be left behind for a while. We read to experience magic. We can escape with Rayel, with Artie, with Putnam, from things that are unbearable—grief or trauma that is too hard to look at straight on.

And yet, as in real life, the escape can also be a way to come to terms with trauma—or at least to begin to. Like Artie, Rayel, and Putnam, we all have bears that follow us. We all have scary things that will not let us go. And sometimes a story, a story with magic and escape and other worlds, can help us see our own very real bears in a new way.

When I wrote *A Crack in the Sea* a few years ago, I was thinking about how we can study history to help us understand our present. I was thinking about how *real* stories, from our *real* collective past, might come together and help us reconsider how we see each other and what it means to leave our birthplace and have to find a new home.

With *A Tear in the Ocean*, I was again thinking about what *home* means—and what it means to feel unwanted in your original home. Artie, Rayel, and Putnam all in their own ways feel unwanted and unloved. While *A Crack in the Sea* was largely about involuntary mass movements of people (people who were enslaved, refugees of war), *A Tear in the Ocean* is about individual choices to leave home—though "choice" in the case of Artie and Rayel is maybe making it sound too easy. They aren't given a lot of other options, not options that keep them safe, anyway.

Instead of bringing in historical events as I did with *A Crack in the Sea*, with *A Tear in the Ocean* I wanted to fold in some of the fairy tales and magical stories that I grew up reading and thinking about—as well as some I learned later in life. Fairy tales were important landmarks to me as I grew up, and they are still the stories that I think of when I consider the various paths my life has taken. And I'm not alone. People often compare friends and relatives to fairy tale and folktale characters; and there are many people who (for example) take online quizzes to see which Harry Potter character or TV show heroine they are most like. We connect ourselves to stories.

But even though I love fairy tales, I didn't want *A Tear in the Ocean* to be a fairy tale retelling. I wanted to think about a *handful* of fairytales at the same time. I wanted to pull a bunch of stories together, to mash together fairy tales, myths, and legends, and make a manticore of a book, part one thing and part another (in the manticore's case: human head, lion body, and scorpion tail). I wanted something strange and familiar at the same time, yet, wholly fantastic. Putnam and Artie and Rayel each have their own fairy tale, and when they come together, they can combine to make a new story—and a new life together.

When I was a kid, my sisters and I had a giant map on our bedroom wall—a print of a watercolor painting by Jaro Hess called *The Land of Make Believe*—that we spent a lot of time studying. In this print, the Shoe Where the Old Woman Lives was located within calling distance of Cinderella's cabin, and Jack the Giant Killer lived right across the road from Old King Cole's castle, while on the horizon one could see the Emerald City of Oz, the Castle of the Giants, and the little house where Here the North Wind Lives—just to name a few places. You could put your finger on the glass and trace the path (which I did, often), traveling the whole mixed-up world, making up stories as you journeyed.

I love a world with so many possibilities for stories.

In *A Tear in the Ocean*, you won't find a map, but you might, as you read, run across strange retellings of (or references to) different fairy tales, folktales, or myths. And you might consider which myths or folktales you'd refer to if you were writing a story. What are the important stories in your own life?

Mostly, though, I hope you read this book and see how brave Artie and Rayel and Putnam are, and how much they've survived. And I hope you can see how much you have survived, and how brave you are.

You know the bear that torments you. You know, too, that

people around you have their own bears to deal with. You know what icy land you travel through. You have some ideas of your powers—or maybe you are still waiting for those powers to be revealed. You have choices to make, journeys to take or to turn back from. And you have people you can travel with, even if you haven't yet met these people.

Books never end. If they mean something to you, they live on in your head, and the story becomes a part of your own life. Your own story, meanwhile, is incomplete. What pulls you forward into the unknown? From whence will you someday return, and as what kind of person?

Our lives are gold-threaded with stories.

Go be a hero in your own story. I know you can.

THANK YOU to Swati Avasthi for reading and commenting on this manuscript, and for telling me to keep working on it, and for hundreds of hours of discussion about writing, reading, and life. Thank you, Swati and Megan Atwood, for insightful comments on this essay. Thank you, Sarah Ahiers, for the eleventh-hour manuscript comments and pep talk. Tricia Lawrence, thank you for your untiring support; you're a truly fantastic agent and friend. Thanks to my brilliant editor Stacey Barney for knowing exactly how to respond to a very messy first draft to keep me revising, and to Courtney Gilfillian for early questions about characters and for timely responses to my own questions. Thank you to Ana Deboo for thoughtful copyediting (and for catching those pesky continuity errors!) and to Jacqueline Hornberger and Rob Farren for proofreading. I'm deeply grateful to the University of St. Thomas for a University Scholar grant that allowed me writing time; I'm grateful, as I have been since I started teaching at St. Thomas, for a department of thoughtful colleagues and friends.

Thank you, thank you, once again to Yuko Shimizu for the amazing art; everything you draw makes me gasp with wonder.

Finally, thank you to my three sisters, with whom I traced out *The Land of Make Believe* and with whom I have shared so many adventures and stories. And thank you to my two beloved sons, my first readers, for whom every book is intended.